...rably drawn

...minded him of his mission here and ...ow ne wasn't any closer to the truth than he'd been when he arrived.

They headed out of the garage. The sky had darkened. He could see distant lightning over the ocean.

"I should warn you we sometimes lose power in the middle of a big storm. You can find emergency candles and matches in the top drawer in the kitchen."

"Thanks." Max headed up the stairs, trying not to favour his stiff ankle, but his efforts were in vain.

"Your ankle! I completely forgot about it! I'm an idiot to make you stand out there for hours just to hold my ladder. I'm so sorry!"

"It wasn't hours, and you're not an idiot. I'm fine. The ankle doesn't even hurt any more."

It wasn't quite the truth but he wasn't about to tell her that.

He didn't want her sympathy.

He wanted something else entirely from Anna Galvez, something he damn well knew he had n...

A Soldier's Secret

RAEANNE THAYNE

MILLS & BOON®

Pure reading pleasure™

*All the characters in this book have no existence outside the
imagination of the author, and have no relation whatsoever to anyone
bearing the same name or names. They are not even distantly inspired
by any individual known or unknown to the author, and all the
incidents are pure invention.*

*First published in Great Britain 2009
by Harlequin Mills & Boon Limited,
Eton House, 18-24 Paradise Road, Richmond, Surrey TW9 1SR*

© Raeanne Thayne 2008

ISBN: 978 0 263 87039 8

23-0509

*Harlequin Mills & Boon policy is to use papers that are
natural, renewable and recyclable products and made from
wood grown in sustainable forests. The logging and
manufacturing processes conform to the legal environmental
regulations of the country of origin.*

*Printed and bound in Spain
by Litografía Rosés S.A., Barcelona*

RAEANNE THAYNE

finds inspiration in the beautiful northern Utah mountains, where she lives with her husband and three children. Her books have won numerous honours, including a RITA® Award nomination from Romance Writers of America and a Career Achievement Award from *Romantic Times BOOKreviews* magazine. RaeAnne loves to hear from readers and can be reached through her website at http://www.raeannethayne.com.

To my brothers, Maj. Brad Robinson,
US Air Force,and high-school teacher
and coach Mike Robinson.
Both of you are heroes!

Chapter One

Lights were on in her attic—lights that definitely hadn't been gleaming when she left that morning.

A cold early March breeze blew off the ocean, sending dead leaves skittering across the road in front of her headlights and twisting and yanking the boughs of the Sitka spruce around Brambleberry House as Anna Galvez pulled into the driveway, behind an unfamiliar vehicle.

The lights and the vehicle could only mean one thing.

Her new tenant had arrived.

She sighed. She *so* didn't need this right now. Exhaustion pressed on her shoulders with heavy, punishing hands and she wanted nothing but to slip into a warm bath with a mind-numbing glass of wine.

The day had been beyond ghastly. She could imagine few activities more miserable than spending an entire humiliating day sitting in a Lincoln City courtroom being confronted with the unavoidable evidence of her own stupidity.

And now, despite her battered ego and fragile psyche, she had to go inside and make nice with a stranger who wouldn't even be renting the top floor of Brambleberry House if not for the tangled financial mess that stupidity had caused.

In the backseat, Conan gave one sharp bark, though she didn't know if he was anxious at the unfamiliar vehicle parked in front of them or just needed to answer the call of nature.

Since they had been driving for an hour, she opted for the latter and hurried out into the wet cold to open the sliding door of her minivan. The big shaggy beast she inherited nearly a year earlier, along with the rambling Victorian in front of her, leaped out in one powerful lunge.

Tail wagging, he rushed immediately to sniff around the SUV that dared to enter his territory without his permission. He lifted his leg before she could kick-start her brain and Anna winced.

"Conan, get away from there," she called sternly. He sent her a quizzical look, then gave a disgruntled snort before lowering his leg and heading to one of his favorite trees instead.

She really hoped her new tenant didn't mind dogs.

She hated the idea of a stranger in Sage's apartment. If she had her way, she would keep it empty, even though Sage and her husband and stepdaughter had their own beach house now a half mile down the shore for their frequent visits to Cannon Beach from their San Francisco home.

But after Anna vehemently refused to accept financial help from Sage and Eben, Sage had insisted she at least rent out her apartment to help defray costs.

The two of them were co-owners of the house and Sage's opinion certainly had weight. Besides, Anna was nothing if not practical. The apartment was empty, she had a fierce, unavoidable need for income and she knew many people were willing to pay a premium for furnished beach-front living space.

Army Lieutenant Harry Maxwell among them.

She gazed up at the lights cutting through the twilight from the third-story window. She was going to have to go up there and welcome him to Brambleberry House. No question. It was the right thing to do, even if the long, exhausting day in that courtroom had left her as bedraggled and wrung-out as one of Conan's tennis balls after a good hard game of fetch on the beach.

She might want to do nothing but climb into her bed, yank the covers over her head and weep for her shattered dreams and her own stupidity, but she had to put all that aside for now and do the polite thing.

She grabbed her laptop case from the passenger seat just as her cell phone rang. Anna swallowed a groan when she saw the name and phone number.

She wasn't sure what was worse—making nice with a stranger now living in her home or being forced to carry on a conversation with the bubbly real estate agent who had facilitated the whole deal.

With grim resignation, she opened her phone and connected the call. "Anna Galvez speaking."

"Anna! It's Tracy Harder!"

Even if she hadn't already noted Tracy's information on the caller ID, she would have recognized the other woman's perky enthusiasm in an instant.

"So have you seen him yet?" Tracy asked.

Anna screwed her eyes shut as if she could just make those upstairs lights—and Tracy—disappear. "I just pulled up to the house, Tracy. I've been in Lincoln City all day. I haven't had a chance to even walk into the house yet. So, no, I haven't seen him. I'm planning to go up to say hello in a moment."

"You are the luckiest woman in town right now. I mean it! You have absolutely *no* idea."

"You're right," she said, unable to keep the dry note out of her voice. "But I'm willing to bet you're about to enlighten me."

Tracy gave a low, sultry laugh. "I know we didn't mention a finder's fee on top of my usual property management commission, but you just might want to kick a bonus over my way after you meet him. The man is gorgeous. Yum, that's all I have to say. *Yum!*"

Just what she needed. A player who would probably be entertaining a long string of model types at all hours of the day and night. "As long as he pays his rent on time and only needs a two-month lease, I don't care what he looks like."

"That's because you haven't met him yet. How much longer will Julia Blair and her kids be renting the second floor? I might be interested when she moves out—I'd love to be beneath that man."

Anna couldn't help her groan, both at Tracy's not so subtle sexual innuendo and at the idea of the real estate agent's wild boys living in the second-floor apartment.

"Julia and Will aren't getting married until June," she answered. With any luck, Lieutenant Maxwell would be long gone by then, leaving behind only his nice fat rental check.

"When she moves out, let me know. That might be a good time for us to talk about a more long-term solution to Brambleberry House. You can't keep taking in temporary renters to pay for the repairs on it. The place is a black hole that will suck away every penny you have."

Didn't she just know it? Anna let herself in the front door, noting that the paint on the porch was starting to crack and peel.

Replacing the furnace the month before had taken just about her last dime of discretionary income—not that she had much of that, as she tried to shore up her faltering business amid scandal and chicanery. The house needed a new roof, which was going to cost more than buying a brand-new car.

"Now listen," Tracy went on in her ear as Anna opened the door to her apartment to set down her laptop, Conan on her heels. "I told you I've got several fabulous potential buyers on the hook with both the cash and the interest in a great old Victorian on the coast. You need to think about it, Anna. I mean it."

"I guess I didn't realize there was such a market for big black holes these day."

Tracy laughed. "When you have enough money, no hole is too big or too black."

And when you had none, even a pothole could feel like an insurmountable obstacle. Anna swallowed another sigh. "I appreciate the offer and your help finding a tenant for the attic apartment."

"But you're not interested in selling." Tracy's voice was resigned.

"Not right now."

"You're as stubborn as Abigail was. I'm telling you, Anna, you're sitting on a gold mine."

"I know." She sat down in Abigail's favorite armchair. "But for now it's my gold mine. Mine and Sage's."

"All right, but when you change your mind, you know where to find me. And I want you to call me after you meet our Lieutenant Maxwell."

As far as Anna was concerned, the man wasn't *our* anything. Tracy was welcome to him. "Thanks again for dealing with the details of the rental agreement," she answered. "I'll let you know how things are going in a week or two. 'Bye, Tracy."

She ended the call and set down her phone, then leaned her head back against the floral upholstery. Conan sat beside her and, like the master manipulator he was, nudged one of her hands off the armrest and onto his head.

She scratched him between the ears for a moment, trying to let the peace she usually found at Brambleberry House seep through her. After a few moments—just when her eyelids were drifting closed—Conan slid away from her and moved to the door. He planted his haunches there and watched her expectantly.

"Yeah, I know, already," she grumbled. "I plan to go upstairs and say hello. I don't need you nagging me about it. I just need a minute to work up to it."

Still, she climbed out of the chair. After a check in the mirror above the hall tree, she did a quick repair of her French twist, grabbed Conan's leash off the hook by the door and put it on him, then headed up the stairs to meet her new neighbor.

As she trailed her fingers on the railing worn smooth by a hundred years of Dandridge hands, she reviewed what she knew about the man. Though Tracy had handled the details, Anna knew Lieutenant Maxwell had impeccable references.

He was an army helicopter pilot who had just served two tours of duty in the Middle East. He was currently on medical leave, recovering from injuries sustained in a hard landing in the midst of enemy fire.

He was single, thirty-five years old and willing to pay a great deal of money to rent her attic for only a few months.

When Tracy told her his background, Anna wanted to reduce the rent. She was squeamish about charging full price to an injured war veteran, but he refused to accept any concession.

Fine, she thought now as she paused on the third-floor landing. But she could still be gracious and welcoming to the man and hope that he would find the healing and peace at Brambleberry House that she usually did.

Outside his door, the scent of freesia curled around her and she closed her eyes for a moment, missing Abigail with a fierce ache. Conan didn't let her wallow in it. He gave a sharp bark and started wagging his tail furiously.

With a sigh, Anna knocked on the door. A moment later, it swung open and she forgot all about being kind and welcoming.

Tracy had told the God's-honest truth.

Yum.

Lieutenant Maxwell was tall—perhaps six-two—with hair the color of aged whiskey and chiseled, lean features. He wore a burgundy cotton shirt and faded jeans with a small, fraying hole below the knee.

He had a small scar on the outside of his right eye that only made him look vaguely piratelike and his right arm was encased in a dark blue sling.

The man was definitely gorgeous, but there was something more to it. If she had passed him on the street, she would have called him compelling, especially his eyes. She gazed into their hazel depths and felt an odd tug of recognition. For a brief, flickering moment, he seemed so familiar she wondered if they had met before.

The question registered for all of maybe two seconds before Conan suddenly began barking an enthusiastic welcome and lunged for Lieutenant Maxwell as if they were lifelong friends.

"Conan, sit," she ordered, disconcerted by her dog's reaction. He wasn't one for jumping all over strangers. Despite his moods and his uncanny intelligence, Conan was usually well-mannered, but just now he strained against the leash as if he wanted to knock her new tenant to the ground and lick his face off.

"Sit!" she ordered, more sternly this time. Conan gave her a disgruntled look, then plopped his butt to the floor.

"Good dog. I'm sorry," she said, feeling flustered. "Hi. You must be Harry Maxwell, right?"

Something flashed in his eyes, too quickly for her to identify it, but she thought he looked uncomfortable.

After a moment, he nodded. "Yeah."

With that single syllable, he sounded as cold and remote as Tillamook Rock. She blinked, not quite sure how to respond. He obviously didn't want to be best friends here, he was only renting her empty apartment, she reminded herself.

Despite Conan's sudden ardor, it was probably better all the way around if they all maintained a careful distance during the duration of Harry Maxwell's rental agreement. He was only here for a short time and then he would probably head back to active duty. No need for unnecessarily messy entanglements.

Taking her cue from his own reaction, she forced her voice to be brisk, professional. "I'm Anna Galvez, one of the owners of Brambleberry House. This is my dog, Conan. I don't know what's come over him. I'm sorry. He's not usually so…ardent…with strangers. Every once in a while he greets somebody like an old friend. I can't explain it but I'm very sorry if his exuberance makes you uncomfortable."

He unbent enough to reach down and scratch the dog's chin, which had the beast's tail thumping against the floor in ecstasy.

"Conan? Like the barbarian?" he asked.

"Actually, like the talk-show host. It's a long story."

One he obviously wasn't interested in hearing about, if the remote expression on his handsome features was any indication.

She tugged Conan's leash when he tried to wrap himself around the soldier's legs and after another disgruntled moment, the dog condescended enough to sit beside her. "I'm sorry I wasn't here when you arrived so I could show you around. I wasn't expecting you for a day or two."

"My plans changed. I was released from the military hospital a few days earlier than I expected. Since I didn't have anywhere else to go right now, I decided to head out here."

How sad, she thought. Didn't he have any family eager to give him a hero's welcome?

"Since I was early, I planned to get a hotel room for a couple days," he added, "but the property management company said the apartment was ready and available."

"It is. Everything's fine. I'm just sorry I wasn't here."

"The real estate agent handled everything."

Not everything Tracy probably *wanted* to handle, Anna mused, then was slightly ashamed of herself for the base thought.

This whole situation felt so awkward, so out of her comfort zone.

"You were able to find everything you needed?" she asked. "Towels, sheets, whatever?"

He shrugged. "So far."

"The kitchen is fully stocked with cookware and so forth but if you can't find something, let me know."

"I'll do that."

Despite his terse responses, Anna was disconcerted by her awareness of him. He was so big, so overwhelmingly male. She would be glad when the few months were up, though apparently Conan was infatuated with the man.

She had a sudden fierce wish that Tracy had found a nice older lady to rent the attic apartment to, but somehow she doubted too many older ladies were interested in climbing forty steps to get to their apartment.

Thinking of the steps reminded her of his injury and she nodded toward the sling on his shoulder. "I'm really sorry

I wasn't here to help you carry up boxes. I guess you managed all right."

"I don't have much. A duffel and a suitcase. I'm only here for a short time."

"I know, but it's still two long flights of stairs."

She thought annoyance flickered in his eyes, as if he didn't like being reminded of his injury, but he quickly hid it.

"I handled things," he said.

"Well, if you ever need help carrying groceries up or anything or if you would just like the name of a good doctor around here, just let me know."

"I'm fine. I don't need anything. Just a quiet place to hang for a while until I'm fit to return to my unit."

She had the impression Lieutenant Harry Maxwell wasn't a man who liked being in any kind of position to need help. She supposed she probably shouldn't be holding her breath waiting for him to ask for it.

"I'm afraid I can't promise you complete quiet. Conan is mostly well-behaved but he does bark once in a while. I should also warn you if Tracy didn't mention it that there are children living in the second-floor apartment. Seven-year-old twins."

"They bark, too?"

She searched his face for any sign of a sense of humor but his expression revealed nothing. Still, she couldn't help smiling. "No, but they can be a little…energetic…at times. Mostly in the afternoons. They're gone most of the day at school and then they're usually pretty quiet in the evenings."

"That's something, then."

"In any case, they won't be here at all for several days. Their mother, Julia, is a teacher. Since they're all out of school right now for spring break, they've gone back to visit her family."

Before Lieutenant Maxwell could respond, Conan broke free of both the *sit* command and her hold on the leash and lunged for him again, dancing around his legs with excitement.

Anna reached for him again. "Conan, stop it right now. That's enough! I'm so sorry," she said to her new tenant, flustered at the negative impression they must be making.

"No worries. I'm not completely helpless. I think I can still manage to handle one high-strung mutt."

"Conan is not like most dogs," she muttered. "Most of the time we forget he even *is* a canine."

"The dog breath doesn't give him away?"

She smiled at his dry tone. So some sense of humor did lurk under that tough shell. That was a good sign. Brambleberry House and all its quirks demanded a strong constitution of its occupants.

"There is that," she answered. "We'll get out of your way and let you settle in. Again, if you need anything, don't hesitate to call. My phone number is right next to the phone or you can just call down the stairs and I'll usually hear you."

"I'll do that," he murmured, his mouth lifting slightly from its austere lines into what almost passed for a smile.

Just that minimal smile sent her pulse racing. With effort, she wrenched her gaze away from the dangerously masculine appeal of his features and tugged a reluctant Conan behind her as she headed back down the stairs.

Nerves zinging through her, Anna cursed to herself as she let herself back in to her apartment. She did *not* need this right now, she reminded herself sternly.

Her life was already a snarl of complications. She certainly didn't need to add into the mix a wounded war hero with gorgeous eyes, lean features and a mouth that looked made for trouble.

* * *

He forgot about the damn dog.

Max shut the door behind the two of them—Anna Galvez and Conan. His last glimpse of the dog was of him quivering with a mix of excitement and friendly welcome and a bit of *why-aren't-you-happier-to-see-me?* confusion as she yanked his leash to tug him behind her down the stairs.

It had been shortsighted of him not to think of Abigail's mutt and his possible reaction to seeing Max again. He hadn't even given Conan a single thought—just more evidence of how completely the news of Abigail's death had knocked him off his pins.

The dog had only been a pup the last time he'd seen him before he shipped to the Middle East for his first tour of duty. During those last few days he had spent at Brambleberry House, Max had played hard with Conan. They'd run for miles on the beach, hiked up and down the coast range and played hours of fetch in the yard.

Had it really been four years? That was the last time he had had a chance to spend any length of time here, a realization that caused him no small amount of guilt.

Conan should have been one of the first things on his mind after he found out about Abigail's death—several months after the fact. He could only blame his injuries and the long months of recovery for sending any thoughts of the dog scattering. It looked as if he was well-fed and taken care of. He supposed he had to give points to the woman—Anna Galvez—for that, at least.

He wasn't willing to concede victory to her, simply because she seemed affectionate to Abigail's mutt.

Anna Galvez. Now there was a strange woman, at least on first impressions. He couldn't quite get a handle on her. She was starchy and stiff, with her hair scraped back in a knot and the almost-masculine business suit and skirt she wore.

He would have considered her completely unappealing, except when she smiled, her entire face lit up as if somebody had just turned on a thousand-watt spotlight and aimed it right at her.

Only then did he notice her glossy dark hair, the huge, thick-lashed eyes, the high, elegant cheekbones. Underneath the layers of starch, she was a beautiful woman, he had realized with surprise, one that in other circumstances he might be interested in pursuing.

Didn't matter. She could be a supermodel and it wouldn't make a damn bit of difference to him. He had to focus on the two important things in his life right now— healing his shattered arm and digging for information.

He wasn't looking to make friends, he wasn't here to win any popularity contests, and he certainly wasn't interested in a quick fling with one of the women of Brambleberry House.

Chapter Two

She could never get enough of the coast.

Anna walked along the shore early the next morning while Conan jumped around in the sand, chasing grebes and dancing through the baby breakers.

The cool March wind whipped the waves into a froth and tangled her hair, making her grateful for the gloves and hat Abigail had knitted her last year. Offshore, the seastacks stood sturdy and resolute against the sea and overhead gulls wheeled and dived in the pale, early morning sky.

It all seemed worlds away from growing up in the high desert valleys of Utah but she loved it here. After four years of living in Oregon, she still felt incredibly blessed to be able to wake up to the soft music of the sea every single day.

Abigail had loved beachcombing in the mornings. She knew every inlet, every cliff, every tide table. She could

spot a California gray whale's spout from a mile away
during the migration season and could identify every bird
and most of the sea life nearly as well as Sage, who was a
biologist and naturalist by profession.

Oh, Anna missed Abigail. She could hardly believe it
had been nearly a year since her friend's death. She still
sometimes found herself in By-the-Wind—the book and
gift store in town she first managed for Abigail and then
purchased from her—looking out the window and expecting Abigail to stop by on one of her regular visits.

*I know the store is yours now but you can't blame an
old woman for wanting to check on things now and again,*
Abigail would say with that mischievous smile of hers.

Anna's circumstances had taken a dramatic shift since
Abigail's death. She had been living in a small two-room
apartment in Seaside and driving down every day to work
in the store. Now she lived in the most gorgeous house on
the north coast and had made two dear friends in the process.

She smiled, thinking of Sage and Julia and the changes
in all their lives the past year. When she first met Sage, right
after the two of them inherited Brambleberry House, she
had thought she would never have anything in common
with the other woman. Sage was a vegetarian, a save-the-
planet sort, and Anna was, well, focused on her business.

But they had developed an unlikely friendship. Then
when Julia moved into the second-floor apartment the next
fall with her darling twins, Anna and Sage had both been
immediately drawn to her. Many late-night gabfests later,
both women felt like the sisters she had always wanted.

Now Sage was married to Eben Spencer and had a new
stepdaughter, and Julia was engaged to Will Garrett and
would be marrying him as soon as school was out in June,
then moving out to live in his house only a few doors down
from Brambleberry House.

Both of them were deliriously happy, and Anna was thrilled for them. They were wonderful women who deserved happiness and had found it with two men she was enormously fond of.

If their happy endings only served to emphasize the mess she had made of her own life, she supposed she only had herself to blame.

She sighed, thinking of Grayson Fletcher and her own stupidity and the tangled mess he had left behind.

She supposed one bright spot from the latest fiasco in her love life was that Julia and Sage seemed to have put any matchmaking efforts on hiatus. They must have accepted the grim truth that had become painfully obvious to her—she had absolutely no judgment when it came to men.

She trusted the wrong ones. She had been making the same mistake since the time she fell hard for Todd Ashman in second grade, who gave her underdog pushes on the playground as well as her first kiss, a sloppy affair on the cheek. Todd told her he loved her then conned her out of her milk money for a week. She would probably still be paying him if her brothers hadn't found out and made the little weasel leave her alone.

She sighed as Conan sniffed a coiled ball of seaweed and twigs and grasses formed by the rolling action of the sea. That milk money had been the first of several things she had let men take from her.

Her pride. Her self-respect. Her reputation.

If she needed further proof, she only had to think about her schedule for the rest of the day. In a few hours, she was in for the dubious joy of spending another delightful day sitting in that Lincoln City courtroom while Grayson Fletcher provided unavoidable evidence of her overwhelming stupidity in business and in men.

She jerked her mind away from that painful route. She

wasn't allowed to think about her mistakes on these morning walks with Conan. They were supposed to be therapy, her way to soothe her soul, to recharge her energy for the day ahead. She would defeat the entire purpose by spending the entire time looking back and cataloguing all her faults.

She forced herself to breathe deeply, inhaling the mingled scents of the sea and sand and early spring. Since Sage had married and moved out and she'd taken over sole responsibility of Conan's morning walks, she had come to truly savor and appreciate the diversity of coastal mornings. From rainy and cold to unseasonably warm to so brilliantly clear she could swear she could see the curve of the earth offshore.

Each reminded her of how blessed she was to live here. Cannon Beach had become her home. She had never intended it to happen, had only escaped here after her first major romantic debacle, looking for a place far away from her rural Utah home to lick her wounds and hide away from all her friends and family.

She had another mess on her hands now, complete with all the public humiliation she could endure. This time she wasn't about to run. Cannon Beach was her home, no matter what, and she couldn't imagine living anywhere else.

They had walked only a mile south from Brambleberry House when Conan suddenly barked with excitement. Anna shifted her gaze from the fascination of the ocean to see a runner approaching them, heading in the direction they had come.

Conan became increasingly animated the closer the runner approached, until it was all Anna could do to hang on to his leash.

She guessed his identity even before he was close enough for her to see clearly. The curious one-handed gait was a clear giveaway but his long, lean strength and brown hair was distinctive enough she was quite certain she would have figured out it was Harry Maxwell long before she could spy the sling on his arm.

To her annoyance, her stomach did an uncomfortable little twirl as he drew closer. The man was just too darn good-looking, with those lean, masculine features and the intense hazel eyes. It didn't help that he somehow looked rakishly gorgeous with his arm in a sling. An injured warrior still soldiering on.

She told herself she would have preferred things if he just kept on running but Conan made that impossible, barking and straining at his leash with such eager enthusiasm that Lieutenant Maxwell couldn't help but stop to greet him.

Maybe he wasn't quite the dour, humorless man he had appeared the day before, she thought as he scratched Conan's favorite spot, just above his shoulders. Nobody could be all bad if they were so intuitive with animals, she decided.

Only after he had sufficiently given the love to Conan did he turn in her direction.

"Morning," he said, a weird flash of what almost looked like unease in his eyes. Why would he possibly seem uncomfortable with her? She wasn't the one who practically oozed sex appeal this early in the morning.

"Hi," she answered. "Should you be doing that?"

He raised one dark eyebrow. "Petting your dog?"

"No. Running. I just wondered if all the jostling bothers your arm."

His mouth tightened a little and she had the impression again that he didn't like discussing his injury. "I hate the sling but it does a good job of keeping it from being shaken around when I'm doing anything remotely strenuous."

"It must still be uncomfortable, though."

"I'm fine."

Back off, in other words. His curtness was a clear signal she had overstepped.

"I'm sorry. Not my business, is it?"

He sighed. "I'm the one who's sorry. I'm a little frustrated at the whole thing. I'm not a very good patient and I'm afraid I don't handle limitations on my activities very well."

She sensed that was information he didn't share easily and though she knew he was only being polite she was still touched that he would confide in her. "I'm not a good patient, either. If I were in your shoes, I would be more than just a little frustrated."

Some of the stiffness seemed to ease from his posture. "Well, it's a whole lot more fun flying a helicopter than riding a hospital bed, I can tell you that much."

They lapsed into silence and she would have expected him to resume his jog but he seemed content to pet Conan and gaze out at the seething, churning waves.

It hardly seemed fair that, even injured as he was and just out of rehab, he didn't seem at all winded from the run. She would have been gasping for breath and ready for a little oxygen infusion.

"It looks like it's shaping up to be a gorgeous day, doesn't it?" she said. "Forecasters are saying we should have clear and sunny weather for the next few days. You picked a great time of year to visit Cannon Beach."

"That's good."

"I don't know if you've had a chance to notice this yet but on one of the bookshelves in the living room, I left you a welcome packet. I forgot to mention it when I stopped to say hello last night."

"I didn't see it. What kind of welcome packet?"

"Not much. Just a loose-leaf notebook, really, with some local sightseeing information. Maps of the area, trail guides, tide tables. I've also included several menus from my favorite restaurants if you want to try some of the local cuisine, as well as a couple of guidebooks from my store."

She had spent an entire evening gathering and collating the information, printing out pages from the Internet and marking some of her favorite spots in the guide books. All right, it was a nerdy, overachiever thing to do, she realized now as she stood next to this man who simmered with such blatant male energy.

She really needed to get a life.

Still, he didn't look displeased by the effort. If she didn't know better, she would suspect him of being perilously close to a surprised smile. "Thank you. That was…nice."

She made a face. "A little over-the-top, I know. Sorry. I tend to be a bit obsessive about those kinds of things."

"No, it sounds perfect. I'll be sure to look through it as soon as I get a chance. Maybe you can tell me the best place for breakfast around here. I haven't had much chance to go shopping."

"The Lazy Susan is always great or any of the B and Bs, really."

Or you could invite him to breakfast.

The thought whispered through her mind and she blinked, wondering where in the world it came from. That just wasn't the sort of thing she did. Now, Abigail would have done it in a heartbeat, and Sage probably would have as well, but Anna wasn't nearly as audacious.

But the thought persisted, growing stronger and stronger. Finally the words seemed to just blurt from her mouth. "Look, I'd be happy to fix something for you. I was in the mood for French toast anyway and it's silly to make it just for me."

He stared at her for a long moment, his eyes wide with surprise. The silence dragged on a painfully long time, until heat soaked her cheeks and she wanted to dive into the cold waves to escape.

"Sorry. Forget it. Stupid suggestion."

"No. No, it wasn't. I was just surprised, that's all. Breakfast would be great, if you're sure it's not too much trouble."

"Not at all. Can you give me about forty-five minutes to finish with Conan's morning walk?"

"No problem. That will give me a chance to finish my run and take a shower."

Now there was a visual she didn't need etched into her brain like acid on glass. She let out a breath. "Great. I'll see you then."

With a wave of his arm, sling and all, he headed back up the beach toward Brambleberry House.

With strict discipline, she forced herself not to watch after him. Instead, she gripped Conan's leash tightly so he wouldn't follow his new best friend and forced him to come with her by walking with firm determination in the other direction.

What just happened there? She had to be completely insane. Temporarily possessed by the spirit of Abigail that Sage and Julia seemed convinced still lingered at Brambleberry House.

She faced what was undoubtedly shaping up to be another miserable day sitting in the courtroom listening to more evidence of her own foolishness. And because she felt compelled to attend every moment of the trial, she had tons of work awaiting her at both the Cannon Beach and Lincoln City stores.

So what was she thinking? She had absolutely no business inviting a sexy injured war veteran to breakfast.

Remember your abysmal judgment when it comes to men, she reminded herself sternly.

It was just breakfast, though. He was her tenant and it was her duty to get to know the man living upstairs in her home. She was just being a responsible landlady.

Still, she couldn't control the excited little bump of anticipation. Nor could she ignore the realization that she was looking forward to the day more than she had anything else since before Christmas, when everything safe and secure she thought she had built for herself crashed apart like a house built on the shifting, unstable sands of Cannon Beach.

This might be easier than he thought.

Fresh from the shower, Max pulled a shirt out of his duffel, grateful it was at least moderately unwrinkled. It wouldn't hurt to make a good impression on his new landlady. So far she didn't seem suspicious of him—he doubted she would have invited him to breakfast otherwise.

Now *there* was an odd turn of events. He had to admit, he was puzzled as all hell by the invitation. Why had she issued it? And so reluctantly, too. She had looked as shocked by it as he had been.

The woman baffled him. She seemed a contradiction. Yesterday she had been all prim and proper in her business suit, today she had appeared fresh and lovely as a spring morning and far too young to own a seaside mansion and two businesses.

He didn't understand her yet. But he would, he vowed.

Not so difficult to puzzle out had been his own reaction to her. When he had seen her walking and had recognized Conan, he had been stunned and more than a little disconcerted by the instant heat pooling in his gut.

Rather inconvenient, that surge of lust. His unwilling attraction to Anna Galvez. He would no doubt have a much easier time focusing on his goal without that particular complication.

How, exactly, was he supposed to figure out if Ms. Galvez had conned a sweet old lady when he couldn't seem to wrap his feeble male brain around anything but pulling all that thick, glossy hair out of its constraints, burying his fingers in it and devouring her mouth with his?

He yanked off the pain-in-the-ass waterproof covering he had to use to protect his most recent cast from yet another reconstructive surgery and carefully eased his arm through the sleeve of the shirt. He was almost—but not quite—accustomed to the pain that still buzzed across his nerve endings whenever he moved the arm.

It wasn't as bad as it used to be. After more than a dozen surgeries in six months, he could have a little mobility now without scorching agony.

He had to admit, he couldn't say he was completely sorry about his unexpected attraction to Anna Galvez. In some ways it was even a relief. He hadn't been able to summon even a speck of interest in a woman since the crash, not even to flirt with the pretty army nurses at the hospital in Germany and then later at Walter Reed.

He had worried that something internal might have been permanently damaged in the crash, since what he had always considered a relatively healthy libido seemed to have dried up like a wadi in a sandstorm.

He had even swallowed his pride and asked one of the doctors about it just before his discharge and had been told not to worry about it. He'd been assured that his body had only been a little busy trying to heal, just as his mind had been struggling with his guilt over the deaths of two members of his flight crew.

When the time was right, he'd been told, all the plumbing would probably work just as it had before.

It might be inconvenient that he was attracted to Anna Galvez, inconvenient and more than a little odd, since he had never been attracted to the prim, focused sort of woman before, but he couldn't truly say he was sorry about it.

And if he needed a reminder of why he couldn't pursue

the attraction, he only needed to look around him at the familiar walls of Brambleberry House.

For all he knew, Anna Galvez was the sneaky, conniving swindler his mother believed her to be, working her wiles to gull his elderly aunt out of this house and its contents, all the valuable antiques and keepsakes that had been in his father's family for generations.

He wouldn't know until he had run a little reconnaissance here to see where things stood.

His father had been the only child of Abigail's solitary sibling, her sister Suzanna, which made Max Abigail's only living relative.

Though he hadn't really given it much thought—mostly because he didn't like thinking about his beloved greataunt's inevitable passing—he supposed he had always expected to inherit Brambleberry House someday.

Finding out she had left the house to two strangers had been more than a little bit surprising.

She must not have loved you enough.

The thought slithered through his mind, cold and mean, but he pushed it away. Abigail had loved him. He could never doubt that. For some inexplicable reason, she had decided to give the house to two strangers and he was determined to find out why.

And this morning provided a perfect opportunity to give Anna Galvez a little closer scrutiny, so he'd better get on with things.

Buttoning a shirt with one good hand genuinely sucked, he had discovered over the last six months, but it wasn't nearly as tough as trying to maneuver an arm that didn't want to cooperate through the unwieldy holes in a T-shirt or, heaven forbid, a long-sleeved sweater, so he persevered.

When he finished, he put the blasted sling on again, ran a comb through his hair awkwardly with his left hand, then headed for the stairs, his hand on the banister he remembered Abigail waxing to a lustrous sheen just so he could slide down it when he was a boy.

Delicious smells greeted him the moment he headed downstairs—coffee, bacon, hash browns and something sweet and yeasty. His stomach rumbled but he reminded himself he was a soldier, trained to withstand temptation.

No matter how seemingly irresistible.

He paused outside Abigail's door, a little astounded at the sudden nerves zinging through him.

It was one thing to inhabit the top floor of Brambleberry House. It was quite another, he discovered, to return to Abigail's private sanctuary, the place he had loved so dearly.

The rooms beyond this door had been his haven when he was a kid. The one safe anchor in a tumultuous, unstable childhood—not the house, he supposed, as much as the woman who had been so much a part of it.

No matter what might be happening in his regular life—whether his mother was between husbands or flushed with the glow of new love that made her forget his existence or at the bitter, ugly end of another marriage—Abigail had always represented safety and security to him.

She had been fun and kind and loving and he had craved his visits here like a drunk needed rotgut. He had looked forward to the two weeks his mother allowed him with fierce anticipation the other fifty weeks of the year. Whenever he walked through this door, he had felt instantly wrapped in warm, loving arms.

And now a stranger lived here. A woman who had somehow managed to convince an old woman to leave her this house.

No matter how lovely Anna Galvez might be, he couldn't forget that she had usurped Abigail's place in this house.

It was hers now and he damn well intended to find out why.

He drew in a deep breath, adjusted his sling one more time, then reached out to knock on Abigail's door.

Chapter Three

She opened the door wearing one of his aunt's old ruffled bib aprons.

He recognized it instantly, pink flowers and all, and had a sudden image of Abigail in the kitchen, bedecked with jewels as always, grinning and telling jokes as she cooked up a batch of her famous French toast that dripped with caramel and brown sugar and pralines.

He had to admit he found the dichotomy a little disconcerting. Whether Anna was a con artist or simply a modern businesswoman, he wouldn't have expected her to be wearing something so softly worn and old-fashioned.

He doubted Abigail had ever looked quite as appealing in that apron. Anna Galvez's skin had a rosy glow to it and the friendly pink flowers made her look exotically beautiful in contrast.

"Good morning again," she said, her smile polite, perhaps even a little distant.

Maybe he ought to forget this whole thing, he thought. Just head back out the door and up the stairs. He could always grab a granola bar and a cola for breakfast.

He wasn't sure he was ready to face Abigail's apartment just yet, and especially not with this woman looking on.

"Something smells delicious in here, like you've gone to a whole lot of work. I hope this isn't a big inconvenience for you."

Her smile seemed a little warmer. "Not at all. I enjoy cooking, I just don't get the chance very often. Come in."

She held the door open for him and he couldn't figure out a gracious way to back out. Doing his best to hide his sudden reluctance, he stepped through the threshold.

He shouldn't have worried.

Nothing was as he remembered. When Abigail was alive, these rooms had been funky and cluttered, much like his aunt, with shelves piled high with everything from pieces of driftwood to beautifully crafted art pottery to cheap plastic garage-sale trinkets.

Abigail had possessed her own sense of style. If she liked something, she had no compunction about displaying it. And she had liked a wide variety of things.

The fussy wallpaper he remembered was gone and the room had been painted a crisp, clean white. Even more significant, a few of the major walls had been removed to open up the space. The thick, dramatic trim around the windows and ceiling was still there and nothing jarred with the historic tone of the house but he had to admit the space looked much brighter. Cleaner.

Elegant, even.

He had only a moment to absorb the changes before a plaintive whine echoed through the space. He followed the sound and discovered Conan just on the other side of the long sofa that was canted across the living room.

The dog gazed at him with longing in his eyes and though he practically knocked the sofa cushions off with his quivering, he made no move to lunge at him.

Max blinked at the canine. "All right. What's with the dog? Did somebody glue his haunches to the sofa?"

She made a face. "No. We're working on obedience. I gave him a strict *sit-stay* command before I opened the door. I'm afraid it's not going to last, as much as he wants to be good. I'm sorry."

"I don't mind. I like dogs."

He particularly liked this one and had since Conan was a pup Abigail had rescued from the pound, though he certainly couldn't tell her that.

She took pity on the dog and released him from the position with a simple "Okay."

Conan immediately rushed for Max, nudging at him with that big furry red-gold head, just as a timer sounded through the room.

"Perfect. That's everything. Do you mind eating in the kitchen? I have a great view of the ocean from there."

"Not at all."

He didn't add that Abigail's small kitchen, busy and cluttered as it was, had always been his favorite room of the house, the very essence of what made Brambleberry House so very appealing.

He found the small round table set with Abigail's rose-covered china and sunny yellow napkins. A vase of fresh flowers sent sweet smells to mingle with the delicious culinary scents.

"Can I do anything?"

"No, everything's all finished. I just need to pull it from the oven. You can go ahead and sit down."

He sat at one of the place settings where he had a beautiful view of the sand and the sea and the haystacks offshore. He poured coffee for both of them while Conan perched at his feet and he could swear the dog was grinning at him with male camaraderie, as if they shared some secret.

Which, of course, they did.

In a moment, Anna returned to the table with a casserole dish. She set it down then removed covers from the other plates on the table and his mouth watered again at the crispy strips of bacon and mound of scrambled eggs.

"This is enough to feed my entire platoon, ma'am."

She grimaced. "I haven't cooked for anyone else in a while. I'm afraid I got a little carried away. I hope you're hungry."

"Starving, actually."

He was astonished to find it was true. The sea air must be agreeing with him. He'd lost twenty pounds in the hospital and though the doctors had been strictly urging him to do something about putting it back on, he hadn't been able to work up much enthusiasm to eat anything.

Nice to know *all* his appetites seemed to be returning.

He took several slices of bacon and a hefty mound of scrambled eggs then scooped some of the sweet-smelling concoction from the glass casserole dish.

The moment he lifted the fork to his mouth, a hundred memories came flooding back of other mornings spent in this kitchen, eating this very thing for breakfast. It had been his favorite as long as he could remember and he had always asked for it.

"This is—" *Aunt Abigail's famous French toast,* he almost said, but caught himself just in time. "Delicious. Really delicious."

When she smiled, she looked almost as delectable as the thick, caramel-covered toast, and just as edible. "Thank you. It was a specialty of a dear friend of mine. Every time I make it, it reminds me of her."

He slanted her a searching look across the table. She sounded sincere—maybe *too* sincere. He wanted to take her apparent affection for Abigail at face value but he couldn't help wondering if his cover had been blown. For all he knew, she had seen a picture of him in Abigail's things and guessed why he was here.

If she truly were a con artist and knew he was Abigail's nephew come to check things out, wouldn't she lay it on thick about how much she adored his aunt to allay his suspicions?

"That's nice," he finally said. "It sounds like you cared about her a lot."

She didn't answer for several seconds, long enough that he wondered if she were being deliberately evasive. He felt as if he were tap-dancing through a damn minefield.

"I did," she finally answered.

Conan whined a little and settled his chin on his fore-paws, just as if he somehow understood exactly whom they were talking about and still missed Abigail.

Impossible, Max thought. The dog was smart but not *that* smart.

"I've heard horror stories about army food," Anna said, changing the subject. "Is it as awful as they say?"

Even as he applied himself to the delicious breakfast, his mind couldn't seem to stop shifting through the nuances and implications of every word she said and he wondered why she suddenly seemed reluctant to discuss Abigail after she had been the one to bring her into the conversation. Still, he decided not to push her. He would let her play things her way for now while he tried to figure out the angles.

"Army food's not bad," he said, focusing on her question. "Army hospital food, that's another story. This is gourmet dining to me after the last few months."

"How long were you in the hospital?"

Just as she didn't want to talk about Abigail, he sure as hell didn't want to discuss his time in the hospital.

"Too damn long," he answered, then because his voice sounded so harsh, he tried to amend his tone. "Six months, on and off, with rehab and surgeries and everything."

Her eyes widened and she set down her own fork. "Oh, my word! Tracy—the real estate agent with the property management company—told me you had been hurt in Iraq but I had no idea your injuries were so severe!"

He fidgeted a little, wishing they hadn't landed on this topic. He hated thinking about the crash or his injuries—or the future that stretched out ahead of him, darkly uncertain.

"I wasn't in the hospital the entire time. A month the first time, mostly in the burn unit, but I needed several surgeries after that to repair my shoulder and arm then skin grafts and so on. All of it took time. And then I picked up a staph infection in the meantime and that meant another few weeks in the hospital. Throw in a month or so of rehab before they'd release me and here we are."

"Oh, I'm so sorry. It sounds truly awful."

He chewed a mouthful of fluffy scrambled eggs that suddenly tasted like foam peanuts. He knew he was lucky to make it out alive after the fiery hard landing. That inescapable fact had been drilled into his head constantly since the crash, by himself and by those around him.

For several tense moments after they had been hit by a rocket-fired grenade as they were picking up an injured soldier that October day to medevac, he had been quite certain this was the end for him and for the four others on his Black Hawk.

He thought he was going to be a grim statistic, another one of those poor bastards who bit it just a week before their tour ended and they were due to head home.

But somehow he had survived. Two of his crew hadn't

been so lucky, despite his frantic efforts and those of the other surviving crew member. They had saved the injured Humvee driver, so that was something.

That first month had been a blur, especially the first few days after the crash. The medical transport to Kuwait and then to Germany, the excruciating pain from his shattered arm and shoulder and from the second- and third-degree burns on the right side of his body…and the even more excruciating anguish that still cramped in his gut when he thought about his lost crew members.

He was aware, suddenly, that Conan had risen from the floor to sit beside him, resting his chin on Max's thigh.

He found enormous comfort from the soft, furry weight and from the surprising compassion in the dog's eyes.

"How are you now?" Anna asked. "Have the doctors given you an estimate of what kind of recovery you're looking at?"

"It's all a waiting game right now to see how things heal after the last surgery." He raised his arm with the cast. "I've got to wear this for another month."

"I can't imagine how frustrating that must be for you. I don't know about you, but I'm not the most patient person in the world. I'm afraid I would want results immediately."

They definitely had that much in common. Though his instincts warned him to filter every word through his suspicions about her, he had to admit he found her concern rather sweet and unexpected.

"I do," he admitted. "But I was in the hospital long enough to see exactly what happened to those who tried to rush the healing process. Several of them pushed too hard and ended up right back where they started, in much worse shape. I won't let that happen. It will take as long as it takes."

"Smart words," she said with an odd look and only then did he realize that it had been one of his aunt's favorite phrases, whether she was talking about the time it took for cookies to bake or for the berries to pop out on her raspberry canes out back.

He quickly tried to turn the conversation back to her. "What about you? For a woman who claims she's impatient for results, you've picked a major project here, renovating this big house on your own."

"Brambleberry House belonged to a dear friend of mine. Actually, the one whose French toast recipe you're eating." She smiled a little. "When she died last year, she left it to me and to another of her lost sheep, Sage Benedetto. Sage Benedetto-Spencer, actually. She's married now and lives in San Francisco with her husband and stepdaughter. In fact, you're living in what used to be her apartment."

He knew all about Sage. He'd been hearing about her for years from Abigail. When his aunt told him she had taken on a new tenant for the empty third floor several years ago, he had instantly been suspicious and had run a full background check on the woman, though he hadn't revealed that information to Abigail.

Nothing untoward had showed up. She worked at the nature center in town and had seemed to be exactly as she appeared, a hardworking biologist in need of a clean place to live.

But five years later, she was now one of the owners of that clean abode—and she had recently married into money.

That in itself had raised his suspicions. Maybe she and Anna had a whole racket going on. First they conned Abigail, then Sage set her sights on Eben Spencer and tricked him into marrying her. What other explanation could there be? Why would a hotel magnate like Spencer marry a hippie nature girl like Sage Benedetto?

"So you live down here and rent out the top two floors?" She sipped her coffee. "For now. It's a lot of space for one woman and the upkeep on the place isn't cheap. I had to replace the heating system this year, which took a huge chunk out of the remodeling budget."

There was one element of this whole thing that didn't jibe with his mother's speculation that they were gold-digging scam artists, Max admitted. If they were only in this for the money, wouldn't they have flipped the house, taken their equity and split Cannon Beach?

It didn't make sense and made him more inclined to believe she and Sage Benedetto truly had cared for Abigail, though he wasn't ready to concede anything at this point.

"The real estate agent who arranged the rental agreement with me mentioned you own a couple of shops on the coast but she didn't go into detail."

If he hadn't been watching her so carefully, he might have missed the sudden glumness in her eyes or the subtle tightening of her lovely, exotic features.

He had obviously touched on a sore subject, and from his preliminary Internet search of her and Sage, he was quite certain he knew why.

"Yes," she finally said, stirring her scrambled eggs around on her plate. "My store here in town is near the post office. It's called By-the-Wind Books and Gifts."

"By-the-Wind? Like the jellyfish?" he asked.

"Right. By-the-wind sailors. My friend Abigail loved them. The store was hers and she named it after a crosswind one year sent hundreds of thousands of them washing up on the shore of Cannon Beach. I started out managing the store for her when I first came to town. A few years ago when she hit seventy-eight she decided she was ready to slow down a little, so I made an offer for the store and she sold it to me."

Abigail had adored her store as much as she loved this house. She wasn't the most savvy of businesswomen but she loved any excuse to engage a stranger in conversation.

"So you've opened a second store now," he asked.

She shifted in her seat, her hands clenching and un-clenching around the napkin in her lap. "Yes. Last summer I opened one in Lincoln City. By-the-Wind Two."

She didn't seem nearly as eager to talk about her second store and he found her reaction interesting and filed it away to add to his growing impressions about Anna Galvez.

He had limited information about the situation but his Internet search had turned up several hits from the Lincoln City newspaper about her store manager being arrested some months ago and charged with embezzlement and credit card fraud.

Max knew from his research that the man was currently on trial. He didn't, however, have any idea at all if Anna was the innocent victim the newspapers had portrayed or if she perhaps had deeper involvement in the fraud.

Before coming back to Brambleberry House, he had been all too willing to believe she might have been involved, that she had managed to find a convenient way to turn her manager into the scapegoat.

It was a little harder to believe that when he was sitting across the table from her and could smell the delicate scent of her drifting across the table, when he could feel the warmth of her just a few feet away, when he could reach out and touch the softness of her skin…

He jerked his mind from that dangerous road. "You must be doing well if you've got two stores. Any plans to expand to a third? Maybe up north in Astoria or farther south in Newport?"

"No. Not anytime in the near future. Or even in the not-so-near future." She forced a smile that stopped just short of genuine. "Would you like more French toast?"

He decided to allow her to sidetrack him for now,

though he wasn't at all finished with this line of questioning. Instead, he served up another slice of the French pastry.

Being here in this kitchen like this was oddly surreal and he almost expected Abigail to bustle in from another part of the house with her smile gleaming even above the mounds of jewelry she always wore.

She wouldn't be bustling in from anywhere, he reminded himself. Grief clawed at him again, the overwhelming sense of loss that seemed so much more acute here in this house.

Oh, he missed her.

He suddenly felt a weird brush of something against his cheek and he had a sudden hideous fear he might be crying. He did a quick finger-sweep but didn't feel any wetness. But he was quite certain he smelled something flowery and sweet.

Out of nowhere, the dog suddenly wagged his tail and gave one happy bark. Max thought he saw something out of the corner of his gaze but when he turned around he saw only a curtain fluttering in the other room from one of the house's famous drafts.

He turned back to find Anna Galvez watching him, her eyes wary and concerned at the same time.

"Is everything okay, Lieutenant Maxwell," she asked.

He shook off the weird sensation, certain he must just be tired and a little overwhelmed about being back here.

Lieutenant Maxwell, she had called him. Discomfort burned under his skin at the fake name. This whole thing just felt wrong somehow, especially sitting here in Abigail's kitchen. He wanted to just tell her the truth but some instinct held him back. Not yet. He would let the situation play out a little longer, see what she did.

But he couldn't have her calling him another man's name, he decided. "You don't have to call me Lieutenant Maxwell. You can call me Max. That's what most people do."

A puzzled frown played around that luscious mouth. "They call you Max and not Harry?"

"Um, yeah. It's a military thing. Nicknames, you know?"

The explanation sounded lame, even to him, but she appeared to buy it without blinking. In fact, she gifted him with a particular sweet smile. "All right. Max it is. You may, of course, call me Anna."

He absolutely was *not* going to let himself get lost in that smile, no matter his inclination, so he forced himself to continue with his subtle interrogation. "Are you from around here?"

She shook her head. "I grew up in a small town in the mountains of Utah."

He raised an eyebrow, certain he hadn't unearthed that little tidbit of information in his research. "Utah seems like a long way from here. What brought you to the Oregon coast?"

Her eyes took on that evasive film again. "Oh, you know. I was ready for a change. Wanted to stretch my wings a little. That sort of thing."

He had become pretty good over the years at picking up when someone wasn't being completely honest with him and his lie radar was suddenly blinking like crazy.

She was hiding something and he wanted to know what.

"Do you have family back in Utah still?"

The tension in her shoulders eased a little. "Two of my older brothers are still close to Moose Springs. That's where we grew up. One's the sheriff, actually. The other is a contractor, then I have one other brother who's a research scientist in Costa Rica."

"No sisters?"

"Just brothers. I'm the baby."

"You were probably spoiled rotten, right?"

Her laugh was so infectious that even Conan looked up

and grinned. "More like endlessly tormented. I was always excluded from their cool boy stuff like campouts and fishing trips. Being the only girl and the youngest Galvez was a double curse, one I'm still trying to figure out how to break."

This, at least, was genuine. She glowed when she talked about her family—her eyes seemed brighter, her features more animated. She looked so delicious, it was all he could do not to reach across the table and kiss her right here over his aunt's French toast.

Her next words quickly quashed the bloom of desire better than a cold Oregon downpour.

"What about you?" she asked. "Do you have family somewhere?"

How could he answer that without giving away his identity? He decided to stick to the bare facts and hope Abigail hadn't talked about his particular twisted branch of the family tree.

"My father died when I was too young to remember him. My mother remarried several times so I've got a few stepbrothers and stepsisters scattered here and there but that's it."

He didn't add that he didn't even know some of their names since none of the marriages had lasted long.

"So where's home?" she asked.

"Right now it's two flights of stairs above you."

She made a face. "What about before you moved upstairs?"

Brambleberry House was the place he had always considered home, even though he only spent a week or two here each year. Life with his mother had never been exactly stable as she moved from boyfriend to boyfriend, husband to husband. Before he had been sent to military school when he was thirteen, he had attended a dozen different schools.

Abigail had been the rock in his insecure existence. But

he certainly couldn't tell that to Anna Galvez. Instead, he shrugged.

"I'm career army, ma'am. I'm based out of Virginia but I've been in the Middle East for two tours of duty. I've been there the last four years. That feels as much home as anywhere else, I guess."

Chapter Four

Oh, the poor man.

Imagine considering some military base a home. She couldn't quite fathom it and she felt enormously blessed suddenly for her safe, happy childhood.

Her family might have been what most people would consider dirt-poor. Her parents were illegal immigrants who had tried to live below the radar. As a result, her father had never been paid his full worth and when he had been killed in a construction accident, the company he worked for had used his illegal immigrant status as an excuse not to pay any compensation to his widow or children.

Yes, her family might not have had much when she was a kid but she had never lived a single moment of her childhood when she didn't feel her home was a sanctuary where she could always be certain she would find love and acceptance.

Later, maybe, she had come to doubt her worth, but none of that stemmed from her girlhood.

And now she had Brambleberry House to return to at the end of the day. No matter how stressful her life might seem sometimes, this house welcomed her back every night, solid and strong and immovable.

It saddened her to think of Harry Maxwell moving from place to place with the military, never having anything to anchor him in place.

"I suppose if you had a wife and children, you would probably be recovering with them instead of at some drafty rented house on the Oregon shore."

"No wife, no kids. Never married." He paused, giving her a careful look. "What about you?"

She had always wanted a big, rambunctious family just like the one she'd known as a girl but those childhood dreams spun in the tiny bedroom of that Moose Springs house seemed far away now.

Her life hadn't worked out at all the way she planned. And though there were a few things in her life she wouldn't mind a do-over on—especially more recent events—she couldn't regret all the paths she had followed that had led her to this place.

"Same goes. I was engaged once but…it didn't work out."

Before he could respond, Conan lumbered to his feet and headed for the door.

"That's a signal," she said with a smile. "Time for him to go out and if I don't move on it, we'll all be sorry. Excuse me, won't you?"

Though he had a doggie door to use when she wasn't home, Conan much preferred to be waited on and to go out through the regular door like the rest of the higher beings. She opened her apartment door and then the main door into the house for him and watched him bound eagerly to his favorite corner of the yard.

When she returned to the kitchen, she found Lieutenant Maxwell clearing dishes from the table.

"That was delicious. It was very kind of you to invite me. A little unexpected, but kind nonetheless."

"You're welcome. I'll be honest, it's not the sort of thing I usually do but…well, it *is* the sort of thing Abigail would have done. She was always striking up conversations with people and taking them to lunch or whatever. I had the strangest feeling this morning on the beach that she would want me to invite you to breakfast."

She heard the absurdity of her own words and made a face. "That probably sounds completely insane to you."

"Not completely," he murmured.

"No, it is. But I'm not sorry. I enjoyed making breakfast and I suppose it's only fitting that I know at least a little about the person living upstairs. At least now you don't feel like a stranger."

"Well, I appreciate the effort and the French toast. It's been…a long time since I've had anything as good."

He gave her a hesitant smile and at the sight of it on those solemnly handsome features, her stomach seemed to do a long, slow roll.

Oh, bad idea. She had no business at all being attracted to the man. He was her tenant, and a temporary one at that. Beyond that, the timing was abysmal. She had far too much on her plate right now trying to save By-the-Wind Two and see that Grayson Fletcher received well-deserved justice. She couldn't afford any distractions, especially not one as tempting as Lieutenant Harry Maxwell.

"I'm glad you enjoyed it," she said, forcing her voice to be brisk and businesslike.

Conan came back inside before he could answer. He

headed straight for the lieutenant, who reached down to pet him. The absent gesture reminded her of another detail she meant to discuss with him.

"I'm afraid I'm going to be tied up in Lincoln City most of today. Some days I can take Conan with me since I have arrangements with a kennel in town but they were full today so he has to stay home. I hope he doesn't make a pest of himself."

"I doubt he'll bother me."

"With the dog door, he can come as he likes. I should probably tell you, he thinks he owns the house. He's used to going up the stairs to visit either Sage when she lived here or Julia and the twins. If he whines outside your door, just send him back downstairs."

"He won't bother me. If he whines, I'll invite him inside. He's welcome to hang out upstairs. I don't mind the company."

He petted the dog with an unfeigned affection that warmed her, though she knew it shouldn't. Most people liked Conan, though Grayson Fletcher never had. That in itself should have been all the red flags she needed that the man was trouble.

"Well, don't feel obligated to entertain him. I would just ask that you close the gate behind you if you leave so he can't leave the yard. He tends to take off if there's a stray cat in the neighborhood."

"I'll do that." He paused. "Would you have any objection if I take Conan along if I go anywhere? He kind of reminds me of a…dog I once knew."

At the sound of his name, the dog barked eagerly, his tail wagging a mile a minute.

Conan would adore any outing, she knew, but she couldn't contain a few misgivings.

"Conan can be a little energetic when he wants to be.

Are you certain you can restrain him on the leash if he decides to take off after a squirrel or something?"

"Because of this, you mean?" he asked stiffly, gesturing to the sling. "My other arm still works fine."

She nodded, feeling foolish. "Of course. In that case, I'm sure Conan would love to go along with you anywhere. He loves riding in the car and he's crazy about any excuse to get some exercise. I'm afraid my schedule doesn't allow me to give him as much as he would like. Here, let me grab his leash for you just in case."

She headed for the hook by the door but Conan had heard the magic word—*leash*—and he bounded in front of her, nearly dancing out of his fur with excitement.

Caught off balance by seventy-five pounds of dog suddenly in her way, she stumbled a little and would have fallen into an ignominious heap if Lieutenant Maxwell hadn't reached out with his uninjured arm to help steady her.

Instant heat leaped through her, wild and shocking. She was painfully cognizant of the hard male strength of him, of his mouth just inches away, of those hazel eyes watching her with a glittery expression.

She didn't think she had ever, in her entire existence, been so physically aware of a man. Of his scent, fresh-washed and clean, of the muscles that held her so securely, of the strong curve of his jawline.

She might have stayed there half the morning, caught in the odd lassitude seeping through her, except she suddenly was quite certain she smelled freesia as she had earlier during breakfast.

The scent eddied around them, subtle and sweet, but it was enough to break the spell.

She jerked away from him before she could do something abysmally stupid like kiss the man.

"I'm sorry," she exclaimed. "I'm so clumsy sometimes. Are you all right? Did I hurt you?"

A muscle worked in his jaw, though that strange light lingered in his eyes. "I'm not breakable, Anna. Don't worry about it."

Despite his words, she was quite certain she saw lines of pain bracketing his mouth. With three older brothers, though, she had learned enough about the male psyche to sense he wouldn't appreciate her concern.

She let out a long breath. This had to be the strangest morning of her life.

"Here's the leash," she said. "If you decide to take Conan with you, just call his name and rattle this outside my door and he should come running in an instant."

He nodded. For a moment, she thought he might say something about the surge of heat between them just now, but then he seemed to change his mind.

"Thanks again for breakfast," he said. "I would offer to return the favor but I'm afraid you'd end up with cold cereal."

She managed a smile, though she was certain it wasn't much of one. He gazed at her for a long moment, his features unreadable, then he headed for the door.

Conan danced around behind him, his attention glued to the leash, but she managed to close the door before the dog could escape to follow him up the stairs.

He whined and slumped against the door and she leaned against it, absently rubbing the dog's ears as that freesia scent drifted through the apartment again.

"Cut it out, Abigail," she spoke aloud. Lieutenant Maxwell would surely think she was crazy if he heard her talking to a woman who had been dead nearly a year.

Still, there had been that strange moment at breakfast when she had been almost positive he sensed something in the kitchen. His eyes had widened and he had seemed almost disconcerted.

Ridiculous. There had been nothing there for him to sense. Abigail was gone, as much as she might wish otherwise. She was just too prosaic to believe Sage and Julia's theory that their friend still lingered here at Brambleberry House.

And even if she did buy the theory, why would Abigail possibly make herself known to Harry Maxwell? It made no sense.

Sage believed Abigail had played a hand in her relationship with Eben, that she had carefully orchestrated events so they would both finally be forced to admit they belonged together.

Though Julia didn't take things quite that far, she also seemed to believe Abigail had helped her and Will find their happily-ever-after.

But Abigail had never even met Harry Maxwell. Why on earth would she want to hook him up with Anna?

She heard the ludicrous direction of her thoughts and shook her head. She had far too much to do today to spend any more time speculating on the motives of an imaginary matchmaking ghost.

She wasn't about to let herself fall prey to any beyond-the-grave romantic maneuvering between her and a certain wounded soldier with tired, suspicious eyes.

Max returned to his third-floor aerie to be greeted by his cell phone belting out his mother's ringtone.

He winced and made a mental note to change it before she caught wind of the song one of his bunkmates at Walter Reed had programmed as a joke after Meredith's single visit to see him in the six months after the crash.

His mother wouldn't be thrilled to know he heard Heart singing "Barracuda" every time she called.

When he was on painkillers, he had found it mildly amusing—mostly because it was right on the money. Now he just found it rather sad. For much the same reason.

He thought about ignoring her but he knew Meredith well enough to be sure she would simply keep calling him until he grew tired of putting her off, so he finally picked it up.

With a sigh, he opened his phone. "Hi, Mom," he greeted, feeling slightly childish in the knowledge that he only used the word because he knew it annoyed her.

She had been insisting since several years before he hit adolescence that he must call her Meredith but he still stubbornly refused.

"Where were you, Maxwell? I've been calling you for an hour." Her voice had that prim, tight tone he hated.

"I was at breakfast. I must have left my phone here."

He decided to keep to himself the information that he was downstairs eating Abigail's French toast with Anna Galvez.

"You said you would call me when you arrived."

"You're right. That's what I said."

He left his sentence hanging between them, yet another strategy he had learned early in his dealings with her mother. She wouldn't listen to explanations anyway so he might as well save them both the time and energy of offering.

The silence dragged on but he held his ground. Finally she heaved a long-suffering sigh and surrendered.

"What have you found?" she asked. "Have those women gutted the house and sold everything in it?"

He gazed around at the apartment with its new coat of paint and kitchen cabinets and he thought of the downstairs apartment, with its spacious new floor plan.

"I wouldn't exactly say that."

"Brambleberry House was filled with priceless antiques. Some of them were family heirlooms that should have gone to you. I can't believe Abigail didn't do a better job of preserving them for you. You're her only living relative and those family items should be yours."

Since she had backed down first, he let her ramble on about the injustice of it all—as if Meredith cared about anyone's history beyond her own.

"I was apparently mistaken to let you visit her all those summers. When I think of the expense and time involved in sending you there, I just get furious all over again."

He happened to know Abigail had paid for every plane ticket and Meredith had looked on those two weeks as her vacation from the ordeal of motherhood but he decided to let that one slide, too.

"She must have been crazy at the end," Meredith finally wound down to say. "That's the only explanation that makes sense. Why else would she leave the house to a couple of strangers when she could have left it to her favorite—and only—nephew?"

"We've had this conversation before," he said slowly. "I can't answer that, Mom."

"What do you intend to do, then? Have you spoken with an attorney yet about contesting the will?"

"It's been nearly a year since Abigail died. I can't just show up out of nowhere and start fighting over the house."

He didn't need Brambleberry House. What did he care about some decaying old house on the coast? He certainly didn't need any inheritance from Abigail. His father had been a wealthy, successful land developer.

Though he died suddenly, he had been conscientious— or perhaps grimly aware of his wife's expensive habits. He had left his young son an inviolable trust fund that Meredith couldn't touch.

Through wise investments over the years, Max had parlayed that inheritance into more money than one man— or ten—could spend in a lifetime.

The money didn't matter to him. Abigail did. She had been his rock through childhood and he owed her at least some token effort to make sure she had been competent in her last wishes.

"You most certainly can fight over it! That house should belong to you, Maxwell. You're entitled to it."

He rolled his eyes. "I'm not entitled to anything."

"That's nonsense," Meredith snapped. "You have far more claim on Brambleberry House than a couple of grubby little gold diggers. Did you contact Abigail's attorney yet?"

He sighed, ready to pull the old bad-connection bit so he could end the call. "I've been in town less than twenty-four hours, Mom. I haven't had a chance yet."

"You have to swear you'll contact me the moment you know anything. The very *moment*."

He had a fleeting, futile wish that his mother had been as concerned when her son was shot down by enemy fire as she apparently was about two strangers inheriting a house she had despised.

The moment the thought registered, he pushed it quickly away. He had made peace a long time ago with the reality that his mother had a toxic, self-absorbed personality.

He couldn't change that at thirty-five any more than he had been able to when he was eight.

For the most part, both of them rubbed together tolerably well as long as they were able to stay out of the other's way.

"I'll do that. Goodbye, Mom."

He hung up a second later and gazed at the phone for a long moment, aware she hadn't once asked about his arm. Just like Meredith. She preferred to pretend anything inconvenient or unpleasant just didn't exist in her perfect little world.

If Brambleberry House had been some worthless shack somewhere, she wouldn't have given a damn about it. She certainly wouldn't have bothered to push him so hard to check into the situation.

And he likely would have ignored her diatribes about the house if not for his own sense of, well, *hurt* that Abigail hadn't bothered to leave him so much as a teacup in her will.

It made no sense to him. She had loved him. Her Jamie, she called him, a nickname he had rolled his eyes at. James had been his father's name and it was his middle name. Abigail seemed to get a kick out of being the only one to ever call him that.

They had carried on a lively e-mail correspondence no matter where he was stationed and he thought she might have mentioned sometime in all that some reason why she was cutting him out of her will.

He had allowed his mother to half convince him Sage Benedetto and Anna Galvez must have somehow finagled their way into Abigail's world and conned her into leaving the house and its contents to them. It now seemed a silly notion. Abigail had been sharp as a tack. She would have seen through obvious gold-digging.

But she was also very softhearted. Perhaps the women had played on her sympathy somehow.

Or maybe she just had come to love two strangers more than she loved her own nephew.

He sighed, disgusted with the pathetic, self-pitying direction of his thoughts.

After spending the last hour with Anna Galvez, he wasn't sure what to think. She seemed a woman of many contradictions. Tough, hard-as-nails businesswoman one moment, softly feminine chef with an edge of vulnerability the next.

It could all be an act, he reminded himself. Still, he

couldn't deny his attraction to her. She was a lovely woman and he was instinctively drawn to her.

Under other circumstances, he might have even liked her.

He heard a vehicle start up below and moved to the window overlooking the driveway. He saw her white, rather bland minivan carefully back out of the driveway then head south toward Lincoln City.

The woman was a mystery, one he was suddenly eager to solve.

Chapter Five

This was a stupid idea.

Just after noon, Max slipped into the condiment aisle of the small grocery store in town, cursing his bad luck—and whatever idiotic impulse had led him to ever think he could get away with assuming a false identity in this town.

He must have been suffering the lingering effects of the damn painkillers. That was the only explanation that made sense.

It had seemed like such a simple plan. Just slip into town incognito, then back out again without anybody paying him any mind.

The idea should have worked. Cannon Beach was a tourist town, after all, and he figured he would be considered just one more tourist.

He had forgotten his aunt had known every permanent

resident in town. Scratch that. Abigail probably had known every single person along the entire northern coast.

He felt ridiculous, hovering among the ketchup and steak sauce and salad dressing bottles. He peeked around the corner again, trying to figure out how he could get out of the store without being caught by the woman with the short, steel-gray hair and trendy tortoiseshell glasses.

Betsy Wardle had been one of Abigail's closest friends. He knew the two of them used to play Bunco on a regular basis. If Betsy recognized him, the entire jig would be up.

He had met her several times before, as recently as four years earlier, the last time he stayed with his aunt.

He couldn't see any way to avoid having her recognize him now. The worst of it was, Betsy was an inveterate gossip. Word would be out all over town that Abigail's nephew was back, and of course that word would be quick to travel in Anna's direction.

He had two choices, as he saw it. He could either leave his half-full grocery cart right here and do his best to hightail it out of the store without being caught or he could just play duck-and-run and try to avoid her until she paid for her groceries and left.

He shoved on his sunglasses and averted his face just in time as she rounded the corner with her cart. He pushed past her, hoping like hell she was too busy picking out gourmet mustard to pay him any attention.

To be on the safe side, he turned in the direction she had just come and would have headed several aisles away but he suddenly heard an even more dreaded sound than Betsy Wardle's soft southern drawl.

Anna Galvez was suddenly greeting the older woman with warm friendliness.

He groaned and closed his eyes. Exactly the last person

he needed to see right now when Betsy could expose him at any second. What was she doing here? Wasn't she supposed to be in Lincoln City right now?

He definitely needed to figure out a way out of here fast. He started to head toward the door when Betsy's words stopped him and he paused, pretending to compare the nutritional content of two different kinds of soy chips while he listened to their conversation one aisle over.

"How is your court case going against that awful man?" Betsy was asking.

"Who knows?" Anna answered with a discouraged-sounding sigh.

"The whole thing is terrible. Unconscionable. That's what I say. I just can't believe that man would work so hard to gain your trust and then take advantage of a darling girl like you. It's just not fair."

"Oh, Betsy. Thank you. I appreciate the support of you and Abigail's other friends. It means the world to me."

He wished he could see through the aisle to read her expression. She sounded sincere but he couldn't tell just by hearing her voice.

"I know I've told you this before and you've turned me down but I mean it. If you need me to testify on your behalf or anything, you just say the word. Why, when I think of how much you did for Abigail in her last years, it just breaks my heart that you're suffering so now. You were always at Brambleberry House helping with her taxes or paying bills for her or whatever she needed. You're a darling girl and I wouldn't hesitate a minute to tell that Lincoln City jury that very thing."

"Thank you, Mrs. Wardle," Anna answered. "While, again, I appreciate your offer, I don't think it will come to that. I'm not the one on trial, Grayson Fletcher is."

"I know that, honey, but from what I've read in the

papers, it sounds like it's mostly his word against yours. I'm just saying I'm happy to step up if you need it."

"You're a dear, Mrs. Wardle. Thank you. I'll be sure to let the prosecutor know."

They chatted for a moment longer, about books and gardening and the best time to plant rhododendron bushes. Just as he was thinking again about trying to escape the store without being identified, he heard Anna say goodbye to the other woman. Out of the corner of his eye, he saw Betsy heading to the checkout counter that was at the end of his aisle.

He turned blindly to head in the other direction and suddenly ran smack into another cart.

"Oh!" exclaimed Anna Galvez.

"Sorry," he mumbled, keeping his head down and hoping she was too distracted to notice him.

No such luck. She immediately saw through the sunglasses. "Lieutenant Maxwell! Hello!"

"Oh. Hi. I didn't see you there," he lied. "This is a surprise. I thought you were going to be out of town today."

Her warm smile chilled at the edges. "My, uh, obligation was postponed for the rest of the afternoon. So instead I'm buying refreshments for one of the teen book clubs that meets after school at By-the-Wind. They're discussing a vampire romance so I'm serving tomato juice and red velvet cake. A weird combination, I know, but they have teenage stomachs so I figured they could handle it."

"Don't forget the deviled eggs."

She laughed. "What a great idea! I wish I'd thought of it in time to make some last night."

When she smiled, she looked soft and approachable and so desirable he forgot all about keeping a low profile. All he wanted to do was kiss her right there next to the organic soup cans.

He jerked his gaze away. "I guess I'd better let you get back to the shopping then. Your vampirettes await."

"Right."

He paused. "Listen, after I'm done here, I was thinking about taking a quick hike this afternoon. I know you said your dog could hang out with me but since you're here, maybe I'd better check that it's still okay with you."

"Absolutely. He'll be in dog heaven to have somebody else pay attention to him."

"Thanks. I'll bring him home about six or so."

"Take your time. I probably won't be done at the store until then anyway."

She smiled again, and it was much more warm and open than the other smiles she'd given him. He could swear it went straight to his gut.

"In truth," she went on, "this will take a big weight off my shoulders. I worry about Conan when I have to work long hours. Sometimes I take him into By-the-Wind with me since he loves being around people, but that's not always the easiest thing with a big dog like Conan. You're very sweet to think of including him."

Sweet? She thought he was *sweet*? He was a lieutenant with the U.S. Army who had been shot down by enemy fire. The last thing he felt was sweet.

"I just wanted a little company. That's all."

He didn't realize his words came out a growl until he saw that soft, terrifying smile of hers fade.

"Of course. And I'm sure he'll enjoy it very much. Have fun, then. I believe there were several area trail guides among the travel information I left in your apartment. If you don't find what you're looking for, we have several others in the store."

"I just figured I would take the Neah-Kah-Nie Mountain trail."

She stared at him in surprise. "You sound like you're familiar with the area. I don't know why, but for some reason, I assumed you hadn't been to Cannon Beach before."

He cursed the slip of his tongue. He was going to have to watch himself or he would be blurting out some of the other hikes he'd gone on with Aunt Abigail over the years.

"It's been a while," he answered truthfully enough. "I'm sure everything has changed since I was here last. A good trail guide will still come in handy, I'm sure. I'll be sure to grab it back at the house before I leave."

"If you get lost, just let Conan lead the way out for you. He'll head for food every time."

"I'll keep that in mind."

He smiled, hoping she wouldn't focus too much on his past experience in Cannon Beach. "Have fun with your reading group."

"I'll do that. Enjoy your hike."

With a last little finger wave, she pushed her cart toward the checkout. He watched her go, wondering how she could manage to look so very delicious in a conservative gray skirt and plain white blouse.

This was a stupid idea, he echoed his thought of earlier, for a multitude of reasons. Not the least of which was the disturbing realization that each time he was with her, he found himself more drawn to her.

How was he supposed to accomplish his mission here to check out the situation at Brambleberry House when all his self-protective instincts were shouting at him to keep as much distance as possible between him and Anna Galvez?

They were late.

Anna sat at her home office computer, pretending to work with her spreadsheet program while she kept one eye out the window that overlooked the still-empty driveway.

Worry was a hard, tangled knot in her gut. It was nearly seven-thirty and she had watched the sun set over the Pacific an hour earlier. They should have been home long before now.

Without Conan, the house seemed to echo with silence. She had always thought that an odd turn of phrase but she could swear even the sound of her breathing sounded oddly magnified as she sat alone in her office gazing out the window and fretting.

She worried for her dog, yes. But she also worried about a certain wounded soldier with sad, distant eyes.

They were fine, she told herself. He had assured her he could handle Conan even at his most rambunctious. He was a helicopter pilot, used to situations where he had to be calm under pressure and he was no doubt more than capable of coping with any difficulty.

Still, a hundred different scenarios raced through her brain, each one more grim than the last.

Anything could have happened out there. Neah-Kah-Nie Mountain had stunning views of the coastline but the steep switchbacks on the trail could be treacherous, especially this time of year when the ground was soaked.

She pushed the worry away and focused on her computer again. After only a few moments, though, her thoughts drifted back to Harry Maxwell.

How odd that it had never occurred to her that he might have visited Cannon Beach before. Is that why he seemed so familiar? Had he come into By-the-Wind at some point?

But if he had, wouldn't he have mentioned it at breakfast when she had talked about buying the store from Abigail?

It bothered her that she couldn't quite place how he seemed so familiar. She usually had a great memory for faces. But thousands of customers walked through By-the-Wind in a given year. There was no logical reason she would remember one man, no matter how compelling.

And he was compelling. She couldn't deny her attraction for him, though she knew it was completely ridiculous.

He was her tenant. That's all she could allow him to be at this complicated time in her life—not that he had offered any kind of indication he was interested in anything else.

Breakfast had been a crazy impulse and she could see now how foolish. It created this false sense of intimacy, as if an hour or so together made them friends somehow, when in reality he had only been at Brambleberry House a day.

No more breakfasts. No more chance encounters on the beach, no more bumping into him at the supermarket. When he and Conan returned safely from their hike—as she assured herself they would—she would politely thank him for taking her dog along with him, then for the rest of his time at Brambleberry House, she intended to do her absolute best to pretend the upstairs apartment was still empty.

It was a worthy goal and sometime later, when her pulse ratcheted up a notch at the sight of headlights pulling into the driveway, she told herself her reaction was only one of relief and maybe a little annoyance that he had left her to worry so long.

She forgot all about keeping her distance, though, when she saw him in the pale moonlight as he gingerly climbed out of his SUV then leaned on Conan as he limped his way toward the house.

Chapter Six

She burst through her apartment into the foyer just as he opened the front door, Conan plodding just ahead of him.

Max looked up with surprise at her urgent entrance, then she saw something that looked very much like resignation flash in his expression before her attention was caught by his bedraggled condition. Mud covered his Levi's and he had a long, ugly scrape on his cheek.

"Oh, my word! Are you all right? What happened?"

He let out a long breath and she thought for a moment he would choose not to answer her.

"I'm fine. Nothing to worry about."

"Nothing to worry about?" she exclaimed. "Are you crazy? You look like you fell off a cliff."

He raised an eyebrow but said nothing and she could swear her heart stuttered to a stop.

"That's not really what happened. Surely you didn't fall off a cliff, did you?"

"Not much of one."

"Not much of one! What kind of answer is that? Either you fell off a cliff or you didn't."

"I slid on a some loose rocks and fell. It was only about twenty feet, though."

Only twenty feet. She tried to imagine falling twenty feet and then calmly talking about it as if she had merely stumbled over a curb. It was too big a stretch for her and her mind couldn't quite get past it.

"I'm so sorry! Did you hurt your arm when you fell?"

He shrugged. "I might have jostled it a little when I was trying to catch a handhold but I managed to stay off it for the most part and land on my left side."

"Please, just tell me Conan didn't trip you or something to make you fall."

He gave a rough laugh and she realized with some shock this was the first time she had heard him laugh. Smile, yes. Laugh, not until just this moment, when he was battered and bleeding and looking like something one of Conan's feline nemeses would drag in.

He reached down to scratch the dog's ears. "Not at all. He was off the leash about five meters ahead of me at the time I slipped. You should be very proud of him, actually. He's a real hero."

"Conan? My Conan?"

"If not for him, I probably would have slipped farther down the scree and gone off the cliff," he answered. "I don't know how he did it, as steep as that thing was, but he made it down the hill where I had fallen and practically dragged me back up, through the mud and the rocks and everything. With my stupid arm and shoulder, I'm not sure I could have climbed back up on my own."

She shuddered at the picture he painted, which sounded far worse than anything she had been conjuring up in her imagination before they arrived home. Twenty feet! It was a wonder he didn't have a couple dozen broken bones!

"I'm so glad you're both okay!"

"I shouldn't be," he admitted. "It was luck, pure and simple. I should never have gone across that rock field. I could tell it wasn't stable but I went anyway. I don't blame you if you don't trust me to take your dog again. But I have to tell you, if not for Conan, I'm not sure I would be here right now. The dog is amazing."

Conan grinned at both of them with no trace of humility. She shook her head, fighting the urge to wrap her arms around her brave, wonderful dog and hold on tight.

"It was lucky you took him, then. And of course you can take him again. Anytime. Maybe he's your guardian angel."

Conan barked as if he agreed completely with that sentiment.

"Or at least helping him out," Max said with a rueful smile.

"You're so certain your guardian angel is a man?"

He made a face. "I haven't really given it much thought. Most women I know would have knocked me to the ground before I could take a step across dangerous terrain in the first place. A preemptive strike, you know?"

"Sounds like you know some interesting women, Lieutenant Maxwell."

"I had an…older relative who taught me most women are interesting if a man is wise enough to allow them room to be."

She blinked. Now there was something Abigail might have said. She wouldn't have expected the philosophy to be echoed by a completely, thoroughly masculine man like Harry Maxwell but she was beginning to think there was more to the helicopter pilot than she'd begun to guess at.

"We could stand out here in the hall having this interesting discussion but why don't you come inside instead and let me help you clean up and put some medicine and bandages on those cuts on your face?"

As she might have predicted, he looked less than thrilled at the prospect. He even limped for the stairs and she felt terrible she had kept him standing even for these few moments.

"Thanks, but that's not necessary. I can handle it."

She raised an eyebrow. "One-handed?"

He paused on the bottom stair with a frustrated sigh. "There is that."

"Come on, Max. I'm happy to do it."

"I don't want to put you to any trouble."

"I had three rough-and-tumble older brothers and always seemed the permanently designated medic. I think I spent half my childhood bandaging some scrape or other. I'm not squeamish at the sight of blood and I have a fairly steady hand with a bottle of antiseptic. You could do worse, Lieutenant Maxwell."

He studied her for a moment, then sighed again and she knew she had won when he stepped gingerly down from the bottom stairs.

"I'm sorry you have to do this. First your dog and now you. The inhabitants of Brambleberry House are determined to look out for me, aren't you?"

Somebody has to do it, she almost said, but wisely held her tongue while Conan barked his own answer as Max followed her into her living room.

Anna Galvez intrigued him more every time he saw her.

Earlier in the grocery store she had worn that slim gray skirt and white blouse with her hair tucked away and had looked as neat and tidy as a row of newly sharpened pencils.

Tonight, as she led the way into her apartment he was entranced by her unrestrained hair as it shivered and gleamed under the overhead lights in a luscious cloud that reached past her shoulders.

She had on the same white blouse from earlier—or at least he thought it was the same one. But she had traded the skirt for a pair of jeans and she was barefoot except for a flirty pair of turquoise flip-flop slippers.

As she led him inside Abigail's apartment, he caught sight of just a hint of pale coral toenail polish peeking through and he found the contrast of that with her slim brown feet enormously sexy.

If he were wise, he would turn right around and race up the stairs as fast as he could go with his now gimpy foot from the ankle he was certain he twisted in the fall.

The hard reality was he wouldn't be going anywhere fast. He hesitated to take off his hiking boot for fear the whole ankle would balloon to the size of a basketball the moment he did. It had ached like crazy the whole way down the mountain and he had a feeling he'd only made it home because his SUV was an automatic and his right leg was fine to work the gas pedal and the brake.

Like it or not, he was stuck in this apartment with Anna for the time being. He could probably do a credible job of washing the worst of the dirt and tiny pieces of mountain from his face but he had a couple of scrapes on his left arm that would be impossible for him to reach very well while the right was still in the damn sling.

It was Anna or the clinic in town and after all the time he'd spent being poked and prodded by medical types over the last six months, Anna was definitely the lesser of two evils.

"Sit down," she ordered in a drill-sergeant sort of voice.

He gave her a mocking salute but was grateful enough to take the weight off his ankle and the throbbing pain. He tried his level best not to wince as he eased onto her couch, feeling a hundred years old, like some kind of damn invalid in a nursing home.

She watched him out of those careful, miss-nothing eyes and he saw her mouth firm into a tight line. He suspected he wasn't fooling her for a moment.

"I just have to gather up a few first-aid supplies and I'll be right back," she said.

"I'm not going anywhere," he answered, which was the absolute truth.

Conan had disappeared into the kitchen—probably to find his Dog Chow, Max figured. If he'd been thinking straight, he should have stopped off and picked up the juiciest, meatiest steak he could find for the hero of the hour.

He leaned back against the sofa cushions and closed his eyes, ready for a little of the calm and peace he had always found in these rooms.

An elusive effort, he discovered, especially since the scent of Anna seemed to surround him here, sweet and sultry at the same time.

He allowed himself the tiny indulgence of savoring that delectable combination for only a moment before she bustled back with her arms loaded down by bandages and antiseptic.

"I don't need all that. Do I really look that terrible?"

She gave him a sidelong look and for just a moment, he sensed something in her gaze that stunned him to the core, a thin thread of attraction that seemed to tug and curl between them.

She was the first one to look away, busying herself with the first-aid supplies. "You want the truth, you look like you just tangled with a mountain lion."

He ordered his pulse to settle down and reminded himself of all the dozens of reasons there could be nothing between them. "Nope," he answered, trying for a light tone. "Just the mountain."

She smiled a little, then reached for the iodine. "Let's take care of the cut on your face first and then I'll check out your arm."

"I can do the face. I just need a mirror for that. I, uh, would appreciate a little help with the arm, though."

For a moment, she looked as if she wanted to argue and he wasn't sure if he was relieved or disappointed when she finally reached for his arm.

Her fingers were deliciously warm on his skin. Sensation rippled from his fingertips to his shoulder and to his vast chagrin, his heartbeat accelerated with the same thick jolt of adrenaline that hit him just as his bird lifted into the air.

Anna was some seriously potent medicine. One touch and he completely forgot about all his other aches and pains.

She gripped his arm firmly with one hand while she used her other hand to dab antiseptic on the scrapes along his forearm. He welcomed the cold, bracing sting of the medicine to counterbalance her heat.

His sudden hunger was a normal response to a lovely woman, he knew. It had been just too long and she was just too pretty for him to sit here without any reaction to her soft curves and silky skin.

"Tell me if I'm hurting you," she said after a moment.

Oh, you have no idea. Max choked down the words.

"Don't worry about it," he muttered instead.

"I mean it. You don't have to be some kind of tough-guy, stoic soldier. If this stings or I'm not careful enough, just tell me to stop."

"I'll be fine," he said gruffly, though it was a bald-faced lie. He couldn't tell her just how badly he wanted to close his eyes and lean into the gentleness of her touch.

What the hell was wrong with him? He had been fussed and fretted over by soft, pretty nurses for the last six months and none of them had ever sparked this kind of reaction in him.

He tried to tell himself it was just a delayed reaction to the adrenaline buzz of his fall—a sort of spit-in-the-face-of-death response. But he wasn't quite buying it.

Her sweep of hair brushed his skin as she bent over his arm and he wondered if she could see the goose bumps rising there.

She didn't appear to notice as she reached for a tube of antibiotic cream and slathered it on with the same slow, careful movements she seemed to do everything.

"You have a choice," she said after a moment.

"Do I?" he murmured.

"I can leave it like this or I can put bandages on the scrapes to protect them for a few days. It's up to you. I would recommend the bandage to keep things clean but it's your decision."

He wanted to tell her to stop but after he had spent several extra weeks in the hospital from a bad infection, he knew he couldn't afford to take any chances.

"Go ahead and wrap it. I might as well look like something out of a horror movie."

She smiled. "Wise choice, Lieutenant."

She pulled out gauze from her kit and wound it carefully around his arm. "If you need me to rewrap this anytime," she said as she worked, "I've got plenty."

"Right."

He figured he'd rather gnaw off his arm than endure this again.

He caught a flicker of movement in the room. Grateful for any distraction, he shifted his gaze and found Conan watching him with what looked like a definite smirk in his eyes, as if he knew exactly how tough this was for Max.

He gave the dog a stern look. *Thanks for the backup.*

When she finished his arm, she stepped back. "Are you sure you don't want me to take care of your face while you're here and all the stuff is out?"

"No. Thanks anyway."

Just the thought of her touching his face with those soft, competent fingers sent shivers rippling through him.

"Anywhere else on you I need to take care of?"

Though his mind instantly flashed a number of inappropriate thoughts, he clamped down on all of them.

"Nope. I'm good. Thanks for the patch job. I appreciate it."

He rose and took only one step toward the door when her voice stopped him.

"You were limping when you came in and you still seem hesitant to put weight on your left foot. What's that all about?"

He turned back warily. "Nothing. I twisted my ankle a little when I fell but it's really fine. Just a little tender."

"You twisted your ankle and then you hiked back down to the trailhead and drove all the way here? Why didn't you say something? We need to put some ice on it."

He had to be the world's clumsiest idiot and right now he just needed to put a little space between himself and the enticing Anna Galvez before he did something he couldn't take back.

"It's really not a big deal. I can take care of it upstairs. You've done enough already."

More than enough. Or at least more than I can handle!

"Oh, stop it! How can you possibly take care of it when you can't use your shoulder?" she pointed out with implacable logic. "I'm willing to bet your foot is swollen enough that you won't be able to even take off your boot by yourself, even if you didn't have your shoulder to contend with as well."

He knew she was right but he wasn't willing to concede defeat, damn it. He'd figure out a way, even if he had to slice the boot off with a hacksaw.

With his eye firmly on his objective—escape—he took another few steps for the door. "You can stop worrying about me anytime now. I can take care of myself."

"I'm sure you can. But you don't always have to," she answered.

He had no response to that so he took a few more steps, thinking if he could only make it to the door, he was home free. She couldn't physically restrain him, not even in his current pitiful condition.

But Abigail's blasted dog had other plans. Before he could take another step, Conan magically appeared in front of him and planted his haunches between Max and the doorway, looking as if he had absolutely no intention of letting him leave the apartment.

He faced the dog down. "Move," he ordered.

Conan simply made a sound low in his throat, not quite a growl but a definite challenge.

"You might as well come back," Anna said, and he heard a thread of barely suppressed laughter in her voice. "Between the two of us, we're here to make sure you take care of that ankle."

He gave Anna a dark look. "Are you really prepared for the consequences of kidnapping an officer in the United States Army, ma'am?"

She laughed out loud at that. "You don't scare me, Lieutenant."

I should, he thought. *I damn well should.*

Once again, he felt foolish for being so churlish when she was only trying to help. He could spend an hour trying to wrestle the boot one-handed or he could let her help him and be done in five minutes.

He sighed. "I would appreciate it if you would help me take off the boot. I can handle the rest from there. I've got ice upstairs."

"Of course. Come back and sit down."

He ignored Conan's look of triumph as he slowly returned to his spot on the sofa. Instead, he cursed his stupid arm and shoulder all over again.

If not for the crash and his subsequent injury, none of this would be happening. He would still be carrying out his duty, he would be flying, he would be in control of his world instead of here in Oregon wondering what the hell he was going to do with the rest of his life.

She knelt on the floor and worked the laces of his hiking boot. Her delicious scent swirled around him again and he told himself the fact that his mouth was watering had more to do with missing dinner than anything else.

Conan seemed inordinately interested in the proceedings. The dog plopped down beside Anna, watching the whole thing out of curious eyes.

The dog was spooky. Max couldn't think of another word for it. Though he felt slightly crazy for even contemplating the idea, he was quite certain Conan understood him perfectly well.

Throughout the day he had carried on a running commentary with him and Conan barked at all the proper places.

He was trying to distract himself, thinking about the dog. It wasn't quite working. He still couldn't seem to avoid noticing the curve of Anna's jawline or the little frown of concentration on her forehead as she tried to ease his tight hiking boot over his swollen ankle.

He jerked his gaze away and his attention was suddenly caught by an open doorway and the contents lined up on shelves inside.

"You kept…" His voice trailed off and he realized he couldn't just blurt out his surprise that she had kept his aunt's extensive doll collection without revealing that he knew about the collection in the first place.

"Yes?"

He couldn't seem to hang on to any thought at all when she gazed at him out of those big dark eyes.

"Sorry. I, um, was just thinking that it, uh, looks like you've kept the original woodwork in the house."

"Actually, not in this room. There was some old water damage and rot issues in here and the trim was beyond saving. I was able to find a decent oak pattern that was a close imitation, though not exact."

"You wouldn't know it's not original to the house."

"I have an excellent carpenter."

"You must have to keep him on retainer with a house of this size."

She made a face, tugging a little harder on the stubborn boot. "Just about. It helps that he only lives a few houses down. And he's marrying Julia Blair, the woman who lives on the second floor."

As she spoke, she finally managed to tug the boot off his ankle.

Before he could jerk his foot away, she rolled the sock down and then gasped. "Oh, Max. That looks horrible! Are you sure it's not broken?"

His entire ankle was swollen to the size of a small cantaloupe and it was already turning a lovely array of colors. He felt like a graceless idiot all over again.

"It's only a little sprain. I just need to wrap it and everything will be fine. Thanks again for your help."

He was determined this time he would make it out of the apartment as he picked up his boot and leaned forward to rise to his feet.

"Max—" she started to argue, and he decided he just couldn't take another word.

Driven by the slow, steady hunger of the last half hour and his own frustration at himself, he bent his head and captured her mouth with his, knowing just a moment's satisfaction that at least he had discovered an effective way of shutting her up.

Okay, it was just about the craziest thing he had ever done in a lifetime of crazy stunts but he couldn't regret it. Not when her mouth was soft and slightly open with surprise and when she tasted like cinnamon and sugar.

Before this moment, he would have thought a kiss where only two sets of lips connected would lack the fire and excitement of a deep, full-body embrace, when he could feel a woman's soft curves against him, the silky smoothness of her skin, each pulse of her heart.

But standing in Anna Galvez's living room with every muscle in his body aching like a son of a bitch, simply touching her mouth with his was the most intense kiss he had ever experienced.

He felt the electrifying heat of it singe through him like a lightning strike, as if he stood atop Neah-Kah-Nie Mountain with his arms outstretched in the middle of a thunderstorm, daring the elements.

Hunger surged through him, a vast, aching need, and he couldn't seem to think straight around it.

This wild heat made no sense to him and contradicted every ounce of common sense he possessed.

If she wasn't a con artist, she was at least an opportunist. She struck him as tight and contained. Buttoned-down, even. Very much not the sort of woman to engage in a wild, fiery romance with a wounded soldier who would be leaving in a few weeks' time.

Despite what logic was telling him, he couldn't ignore

her reaction to his kiss. Instead of jerking away—or even slapping his face—she made a breathy kind of sound and leaned in closer.

That tiny gesture was all it took to send his control out the window and he pulled her closer, suddenly desperate for more.

Chapter Seven

Some tiny, logical corner of her brain that could still function knew this was completely insane.

What was she thinking to be here kissing Harry Maxwell—she barely knew him, he was her tenant, and right now the man couldn't even stand upright, for heaven's sake!

Usually she tried to listen to that common-sense corner of her mind but right now she found it impossible to focus on anything but the heat of him and his strong, commanding mouth on hers.

As he pulled her closer, she wrapped her arms around his waist. This was a little like she imagined it would feel to stand in the midst of the battering force of a hurricane, holding tight to the hard, immovable strength of a centuries-old lighthouse. His body was all heat and hard muscles and she wanted to lean into him and not let go.

She closed her eyes and savored the taste of him, heady

and male, and the thrum of her blood as his mouth explored hers.

The house faded around her and she was lost to everything but the moment. Right now she wasn't a struggling businesswoman or an out-of-her-league homeowner. She wasn't a failure or the victim of fraud or an unwilling dupe.

She was only Anna and at this frozen moment in time she felt beautiful and feminine and *wanted*.

She didn't know how long they kissed, wrapped together in her living room with the sounds of their mingled breathing and the creaks and sighs of the old house settling around them.

She would have been quite willing to stand there forever. But that still-functioning corner of her mind was aware of him shifting his weight slightly and then of his sudden discordant intake of breath.

Awareness washed over her like the bitter cold of a January sneaker wave and she froze, blinking out of what felt like a particularly delicious dream into harsh reality.

What was wrong with her? He was a stranger, for heaven's sake! She'd known him for all of twenty-four hours and here she was entangled in his arms.

She knew nothing about this man other than that he could be kind to her dog and he disliked being fussed over.

This absolutely was not like her. She always tried to be so careful with men, taking her time to get to know them, to give careful thought to a man's positive and negative attributes before even considering a date with him.

And wasn't that course of action working out just great for her? a snide little voice sneered in her mind.

She pushed it away. She barely knew the man. Not only that, but he was injured! He could barely stand up and here she was throwing herself at him. She couldn't even bring herself to meet his gaze, mortified at her instant, feverishly inexplicable reaction to a simple kiss.

Why had he kissed her, though? That was the real question. One moment she had been urging him to take it easy with his sprained ankle—okay, nagging him—and the next moment his mouth had been stealing her breath, and whatever good sense she possessed along with it.

This sort of thing did *not* happen to her.

Still, she found some consolation that he looked as baffled and thunderstruck as she was.

In fact, the only one in the room who didn't look like the house had just imploded around them all was Conan, who sat watching the two of them with an expression that bordered on smug delight, oddly enough.

Max was the first one to break the awkward silence.

"Well, your nursing methods might be a little unorthodox, but I suddenly feel a hell of a lot better."

Her flush deepened. "I'm so sorry. I don't know what…I shouldn't have…"

He held up a hand. "Stop. I was trying to make a stupid joke. I completely started it, Anna. I kissed you. You have nothing to apologize about."

She tried to remember the steps in the circle breathing Sage was always trying to make her practice but her mind was too scrambled to focus on the calming method. She also still couldn't quite force herself to meet his gaze.

"I was way out of line," he added. "I don't know quite what to say, other than you can be sure it won't happen again."

"It won't?" Now why did that make her feel so blasted depressed?

"I don't make it a habit of accosting people who are only trying to help me."

"You didn't accost me," she mumbled. "It was just a kiss."

Just a kiss that still seemed to sing through her body,

moments later. A kiss she could still taste on her lips and feel in her racing pulse.

"Right," he said after a moment. "Uh, I'd better get out of your way and let you get back to…whatever you were doing before we showed up."

She fiercely wanted him gone so she could try to regain a little badly needed equilibrium. At the same time, she couldn't help worrying about his injuries.

"Are you sure you'll be able to make it up the stairs?"

"Unless Conan stands in my way again."

"He won't," she promised. If she had to, she would lock the dog in her bedroom to keep him from causing any more trouble.

He paused at her door. "Good night, then. And thank you again for all your help."

A shadow of something hot and intense still lingered in the hazel depths of his eyes.

She told herself she shouldn't be flattered by it. But her ego had taken a beating the last few months with the trial and Gray Fletcher's perfidy. She felt stupid and incompetent and ugly in the knowledge that Gray had only pursued her so arduously to distract her from his shady dealings at her company—and that she had been idiot enough to fall for it.

Harry Maxwell didn't work for her, he didn't want anything from her. He seemed as discomfited by the heat they generated as she was.

At the same time, the fact that this gorgeous man was at least interested enough in her to kiss her out of the blue with such heat and passion was a soothing balm to her scraped psyche.

He grabbed his boot and headed into the foyer. Though she knew his ankle had to be killing him, he barely limped as he headed up the stairs.

Abigail would have followed him right upstairs with

cold compresses and ibuprofen for his ankle, no matter what the stubborn man might have to say about it.

But Anna wasn't Abigail. She never could be. Yes, she might invite the man over to breakfast to make him feel more welcome in Cannon Beach and she might fill his room with guidebooks and put a little first-aid ointment on his scrapes.

But Abigail had possessed unfailing instincts about people. She didn't make the kinds of mistakes Anna did, putting her trust in the completely wrong people who invariably ended up hurting her....

Though she knew he wouldn't appreciate her concern, she waited until she heard the door close up on the third floor before returning to her living room.

She closed the door and sagged into Abigail's favorite chair, ignoring Conan's interested look as she pressed a hand to her mouth.

What just happened here? She had no idea a simple kiss could be so devastatingly intense.

She had certainly kissed men before. She'd been engaged, for heaven's sake. She had enjoyed those kisses and even the few times she and her fiancé had gone further than kisses.

But she had always thought something was a little wrong with her in that department. While she enjoyed the closeness, she had never experienced the raw, heart-pounding desire, the wild churn in her stomach, that other women talked about.

Until tonight.

Just another reason why her reaction to a wounded soldier was both unreasonable and dangerous. She wanted to throw every caution to the wind and just enjoy the moment with him.

How on earth was she going to make it through the next few months with him living just upstairs?

Julia and the twins would be back in a week. Their presence would at least provide a buffer between her and Max.

Whether she wanted it or not.

She didn't see Max Saturday morning before she left for the store. His SUV was gone and the lights were off on the third floor, she saw with some relief as she backed her van out through a misting rain that clung to her windshield and shimmered on the boughs of the Sitka spruce around Brambleberry House.

He must have left while she was in the shower, since his vehicle had been parked in the driveway next to hers when she returned with Conan from their morning walk on the beach earlier.

She spent a moment as she drove to By-the-Wind wondering where he might have gone for the day. Maybe the Portland Saturday Market? That was one of her favorite outings when she had the time and she was almost certain this was the opening weekend of the season. But would Lieutenant Maxwell really enjoy wandering through stalls of produce and flowers and local handicrafts? She couldn't quite imagine it.

Whatever he had chosen to do with his Saturday was none of her business, she reminded herself. She only hoped he didn't overdo.

She had fretted half the night that he wouldn't be able to get up and down the stairs with his ankle, that he would be trapped up on the third floor with no way of calling for help.

It was ridiculous, she knew. The man was a trained army helicopter pilot who had survived a crash, for heaven's sake, and she had no idea what else during his service in the Middle East. A twisted ankle was probably nothing to someone who had spent several months in the hospital recovering from his injuries.

Her worry was obviously all for nothing. With no help whatsoever from her or Conan, he had managed to get down the stairs, obviously, and even behind the wheel of his vehicle.

Since he was apparently mobile, she needed to stop worrying about the man, especially since she had a million other things within her control she could be stressing over.

She barely had time to even think about Max through-out the morning. Helen Lansing, her wonderful assistant manager who led the weekly preschool story hour on Saturday mornings—complete with elaborate puppets and endless energy—called in tears, with a terrible migraine.

"Don't worry about it," Anna told her as she mentally reshuffled her day. "Just go lie down in a quiet, dark room until you feel better. Michael and I can handle story hour."

The rain—or probably their parents' cabin fever—brought a larger than average crowd to the story hour. It might have been not quite as slick and polished as Helen's shows usually were but the children still seemed to enjoy it—and as a business owner, she certainly enjoyed the sales generated by their parents as they waited for their little ones.

By the time the last child left just before lunch, she was ready for a little quiet.

"I'll be in the office for a few moments working on invoices," she told Michael and Kae, her two clerks. "Yell if you need help."

She had just settled into her desk chair when her office phone rang. She didn't recognize the number and she answered rather impatiently.

"Sorry. Is this a bad time?"

Her mood instantly lifted at the voice on the other end of the line. "Sage! No, of course it's not a bad time. It's never a bad time when you call. How are you? How are Eben and Chloe?"

There was an odd delay on the line, as if the signal had to travel a long distance, though the reception was clear enough.

"Wonderful. Guess where I'm calling from?"

Eben owned a chain of hotels around the world and he and Sage frequently traveled between them, taking his daughter, Chloe.

Last month Sage had called her from Denmark and the month before had been Japan.

"Um, New York City?" she guessed.

"A little farther south. We're in Patagonia!"

"Really? I didn't know Spencer Hotels had a location down there."

"We don't. But Eben's considering it. He wants to capitalize on the high-end ecotourism trend so we're scouting locations. Chloe is having a blast. Just yesterday we went horseback riding through scenery so incredible, you can't imagine. You should have seen her up on that horse, just like she's been riding her whole life."

Sage's love for her stepdaughter warmed Anna's heart. When she and Sage inherited Brambleberry House, she used to be so envious of Sage for her vivid, outgoing personality.

Sage was much like Abigail in that every time she walked into a room, she walked out of it again with several new friends.

Anna never realized until they had become close friends how Sage's exuberance masked a deep loneliness.

That was gone now. Sage and Eben—and Chloe—were genuinely happy together.

"Sounds like you're having a wonderful time."

"We are. And how are things there? What's going on with the trial? I tried to call a few times last week to check in and got your voice mail."

"I know. I got your message. I'm sorry I haven't called you back. I've just been busy…"

Her voice trailed off and she sighed, unable to lie to her friend. "Okay, truth. I purposely didn't call you back."

"Ouch. Screening my calls now?"

"Of course not. You know I love you. I just…I didn't really want to talk about the trial," she finally admitted.

"That bad?"

The sympathy in Sage's voice traveled all the way across the phone line from Patagonia and tears stung behind her eyes.

"Not at all, if you enjoy public humiliation."

"Oh, honey. I'm so sorry. I should have been there. I've been thinking all week that I should have just ignored you when you said you didn't want either Julia or me to come with you. You're always so blasted independent but sometimes you need to have a friend in your corner. I should have been there."

"Completely not necessary. We're on the homestretch now. The defense should wrap up Monday, with closing arguments Tuesday, and a verdict sometime after that."

"I'm coming home," she said after that short delay. "I should be there with you, at least for the verdict."

"You absolutely are not!"

"You're my friend. I can't let you go through this on your own, Anna."

"I can handle it."

She would rather have her tongue chopped into little pieces than admit to Sage how very much she longed for her friends to lean on right now.

"You handle everything. I know. And usually you do a marvelous job at it. But you shouldn't have to bear this burden by yourself."

"If you cut short your dream trip to Patagonia with your

family on my account, I will never forgive you, Sage Bene-detto-Spencer. I mean it. You and Eben have already done more than enough."

"I should be there."

"You should be exactly where you are, horseback riding through incredible scenery with your husband and daughter."

Sage was silent for a moment and Anna thought perhaps the tenuous connection had been severed. "And you have to deal with a new tenant in the middle of all this, too. He's arriving any day now, isn't he?"

She rolled a pencil between her fingers. "Actually, he showed up a few days ago."

"And…?" Sage prompted.

"And what?" she said, stalling.

"What's he like?"

She had a wild, visceral image of his mouth on hers, of those strong muscles surrounding her, of his skin, warm and hard beneath her exploring fingertips.

How should she answer that? He was gorgeous and stubborn and infuriating and his kiss was magic.

"I don't really know. He's only been there a few days. So far everything has been…fine."

It was a vast understatement and she could only be grateful Sage was thousands of miles away and not watching her out of those knowing eyes of hers that missed nothing.

"Any sign of Abigail since your wounded soldier showed up or is she giving him a wide berth?"

"No ghostly manifestations, no. Everything has been quiet on the paranormal front."

"What about Conan? Does he like him?"

"Well, he did try to attack him last night in my apart-ment, but other than that, they get along fine."

"Excuse me? He attacked him? Our fierce and mighty watchdog Conan, who would probably lick an intruder to death?"

She sighed, wishing she'd kept her big mouth shut. Sage was far too perceptive and Anna had a sudden suspicion she would read far more into the situation.

"He and Conan went hiking yesterday on Neah-Kah-Nie Mountain and Lieutenant Maxwell fell and was scraped up a bit. He's already got an injury from a helicopter crash so it was hard for him to tend his wounds by himself but he's the, uh, prickly, independent type. He wasn't thrilled about me having to bandage his cuts. But Conan and I can both be persuasive."

"Okay, now things are getting interesting. Forget some stupid old trial. Now I want to know everything about the new tenant. Tell me more."

"There's nothing to tell, Sage. I promise."

Other than that she had kissed him and made of fool of herself over him and then spent the night wrapped in feverish dreams that left her achy and restless.

"What does he look like?"

Anna closed her eyes and was chagrined when his image appeared, hazel eyes and dark hair and too-serious mouth.

"He looks like he's been in a hospital too long and is hungry for fresh air and sunlight. Conan adores him and is already extremely protective of him. That's what last night was about. Conan didn't want him to go up the stairs until I'd taken a look at his swollen ankle."

"And did you? Get a good look, I mean?"

Better than she should have. "Sage, drop it. There's nothing between me and Lieutenant Maxwell. I'm not interested in a relationship right now. I can't afford to be. When would I have the time, for heaven's sake, even if I had the energy? Besides, I obviously can't be trusted to pick out a decent man for myself since my judgment is so abysmal."

"That's why you need to let Abigail and Conan do it for you. Look how well things turned out for Julia and for me?"

Anna laughed, feeling immeasurably better about life, as she always did after talking to Sage. "So what you're saying is that a fictitious octogenarian spirit and a mixed-breed mutt have better taste in men than I do. Okay. Good to know. If I ever decide to date again—highly doubtful at this point in my life—I'll bring every man home to Brambleberry House before the second date."

They talked a few moments longer, then she heard Chloe calling Sage's name. "You'd better go. Thanks for calling, Sage. I promise, I'll call you as soon as I know anything about the verdict."

"Are you sure you don't want me there?"

"Absolutely positive. When you and Eben and Chloe come back to Cannon Beach at Easter, we'll have an all-nighter and we can read the court transcripts together."

"Ooh, can we do parts? I've got the perfect voice for that weasel Grayson Fletcher."

She pitched her voice high and nasal, not at all like Gray's smooth baritone, but it still made Anna laugh. "Deal. I'll see you then."

She hung up the phone a few moments later, her heart much lighter as she focused on all the wonderful ways her life had changed in the last year.

Yes, she'd had a rough few months and the trial was excruciatingly humiliating.

But she had many more blessings than hardships. She considered Sage the very best gift Abigail had bequeathed to her after her death. Better than the house or the garden or all the antique furniture in the world.

The two of them had always had a cool relationship

while Abigail was alive, perhaps afflicted by a little subtle rivalry. Both of them had loved Abigail and perhaps had wanted her affection for themselves.

Being forced to live together in Brambleberry House had brought them closer and they had found much common ground in their shared grief for their friend. She now considered Sage and Julia Blair her richest blessings, the two best friends she'd ever known.

She had a beautiful home on the coast, she had close friends who loved and supported her, she had two businesses she was working to rebuild.

The last thing she needed was a wounded soldier to complicate things and leave her aching for all she didn't have.

Chapter Eight

Few things could send his blood pumping like a heavy storm roiling in off the ocean.

Max walked along the wide sandy beach with Conan on his leash, watching the churn of black-edged clouds way out on the far horizon. Even from here, he could see the froth of the sea, a writhing mass of deep, angry green.

It wouldn't be here for some time yet but the air had that expectant quality to it, as if everything along the coast was just waiting. Already the wind had picked up and the gulls seemed frantic as they soared and dived through the sky, driven by an urgency to fill their stomachs and head for shelter somewhere.

At moments like this, Max sometimes wondered if he should have picked a career in the coast guard.

He could have flown helicopters there, swift, agile little Sikorsky Jayhawks, flying daredevil rescues on the ocean while waves buffeted the belly of his bird.

He had always loved the ocean, especially *this* ocean—its moods and its piques and the sheer magnificence of it.

Conan sniffed at a clump of seaweed and Max paused to let him take his time at it. Though he didn't want to admit it, he was grateful for the chance to rest for a moment.

Considering his body felt as if it had been smashed against the rocks at the headland, he figured he was doing pretty well. A run had been out of the question, with his ankle still on the swollen side, but a walk had helped loosen everything up and he felt much better.

The ocean always seemed to calm him. He used to love to race down from the house the moment Abigail returned to Brambleberry House from picking him up at the airport in Portland. She would follow after him, laughing as he would shuck off his shoes and socks for that first frigid dip of his toes in the water.

Max couldn't explain it, but some part of him was connected to this part of the planet, by some invisible tie binding him to this particular meshing of land and sea and sky.

He had traveled extensively around the world during his youth as his mother moved from social scene to social scene—in the days before Meredith sent him to military school. He had served tours of duty in far-flung spots from Latin America to Germany to the gulf and had seen many gorgeous places in every corner of the planet.

But no place else ever filled him with this deep sense of homecoming as he found here on the Oregon coast.

He didn't quite understand it, especially since he had spent much longer stretches of time in other locations. When people in social or professional situations asked him where he was from, as Anna had done at breakfast the other day, he always gave some vague answer about moving around a lot when he was kid.

But in his heart, when he thought about home, he thought of Brambleberry House and Cannon Beach.

He sighed. Ridiculous. It wasn't his. Abigail had decided two strangers deserved the place more and at this point he didn't think he could do a damn thing about it.

If his military career was indeed over, he was going to have to consider his options. Maybe he would just buy a fishing boat and a little house near Yachats or Newport and spend his days out on the water.

It wasn't a bad scenario. So why couldn't he drum up a little more enthusiasm for it, or for any of the other possibilities he'd been trying to come up with since doctors first dared suggest he might not ever regain full use of his arm?

He flexed his shoulder as he watched the gulls struggle against the increasing wind. They ought to just give up now, he thought, before the wind made it impossible for them to fly. But they kept at it. Indeed, they seemed to revel in the challenge.

He sighed as his ankle throbbed from being in one place too long. He felt weaker than a damn seagull in that headwind right now.

"Come on, Conan. We'd better head back."

The dog made a definite face at him but gave one last sniff in the sand and followed as Max led the way back up the beach toward Brambleberry House.

The storm clouds were edging closer and he figured they had maybe an hour before the real fun started.

Good. Maybe a hard thunder-bumper would drive this restlessness out of him.

He was grateful for his fleece jacket now as the temperature already seemed to have dropped a dozen degrees or more, just in the time since they set off.

The moment he opened the beach access gate at Brambleberry House, Conan bounded inside, barking like crazy as if he had been gone for months.

Max managed to control him enough to get the leash off and the dog jumped around with excitement.

"You like storms, too, don't you? I bet they remind you of Aunt Abigail, right?"

The dog barked in that spooky way he had of acting as if he understood every word, then he took off around a corner of the house.

As Max followed more slowly, branches twisted and danced in the swell of wind, a few scraping the windows on the upper stories of the house.

He planned to start a fire in the fireplace, grab the thriller he had been trying to focus on and settle in for the evening with a good book and the storm.

Yeah, it probably would sound tame to the guys in his unit but right now he could imagine few things more enjoyable.

A quick image of kissing Anna Galvez while the storm raged around them flashed through his mind but he quickly suppressed it. Their kiss had been a one-time-only event and he needed to remember that.

"Conan? Where'd you go, bud?" he called.

He rounded the corner of the house after the dog, then stopped dead. His heart seemed to stutter in his chest at the sight of Anna atop a precarious-looking wooden ladder, a hammer in her hand as she stretched to fix something he couldn't see from this angle.

The first thought to register in his distinctly male brain was how sexy she looked with a leather tool belt low on her hips and her shirt riding up a little as she raised her arms.

The movement bared just the tiniest inch of skin above her waistband, a smooth brown expanse that just begged for his touch.

The second, more powerful emotion was sheer terror as

he noted just how far she was reaching above the ladder—
and how precarious she looked up there fifteen feet in the air.

"Have you lost your ever-loving mind?"

She jerked around at his words and to his dismay, the
ladder moved with her, coming away at least an inch or
more from the porch where it was propped.

At the last moment, she grabbed hold of the soffit to sta-
bilize herself and the ladder, and Max cursed his sudden
temper. If she fell because he had impulsively yelled at her,
he would never forgive himself.

"I don't believe I have," she answered coolly. "My ever-
loving mind seems fairly intact to me just now."

"You might want to double-check that, ma'am. That
wind is picking up velocity with each passing second. It
won't take much for one good gust to knock that ladder
straight out from under you, then where will you be?"

"No doubt lying bleeding and unconscious at your feet,"
she answered.

He was not going about this in the correct way, he
realized. He had no right to come in here and start issuing
orders like she was the greenest of recruits.

He had no right to do anything here. He ought to just
let her break her fool neck—but the thought of her, as she
had so glibly put it, lying bleeding and unconscious at his
feet filled him with an odd, hollow feeling in his gut that
he might have called panic under other circumstances.

"Come on down, Anna," he cajoled. "It's really too
windy for you to be safe up there."

"I will. But not quite yet."

He wasn't getting her down from there short of toppling
the ladder himself, he realized. And with a bad ankle and
only one usable arm right now—and that one questionable
after the scrapes and bruises of the day before—he couldn't
even offer to take her place.

"Can I at least hold the ladder for you?"

"Would you?" she asked, peering down at him with delight. "I'm afraid I'm not really fond of heights."

She was afraid of heights? He stared at her and finally noticed the slight sheen of sweat on her upper lip and the very slightest of trembles in her knees.

A weird softness twisted through his chest as he thought of the courage it must be taking her to stand there on that ladder, fighting down her fears.

"And so to cure your phobia, you decided to stand fifteen feet above the ground atop a rickety wooden ladder in the face of a spring storm. Makes perfect sense to me."

She made a face, though she continued hammering away. "Ha ha. Not quite."

"Well, what's so important it can't wait until after the storm?"

"Shingles. Loose ones." She didn't pause a moment in her hammering. "We need a new roof. The last time we had a big storm, the wind curled underneath some loose singles on the other side of the house and ended up lifting off about twenty square feet of roof. The other day I noticed some loose shingles on this side so I just want to make sure we don't see the same thing happen."

"Couldn't you find somebody else to do that for you?"

She raised an eyebrow. "Any suggestions, Lieutenant Maxwell?"

"You could have asked me."

She finally stopped hammering long enough to look down at him, her gaze one of astonishment as she looked first at his arm in the blasted sling, then at his ankle.

He waited for some caustic comment about his current physical limitations. Instead, her lovely features softened as if he'd handed her an armload of wildflowers.

"I…thank you," she said, her voice slightly breathless.

"That's very kind but I'm sort of in the groove now. I think I can handle it. I would appreciate your help holding the ladder while I check a couple of shingles on the porch on the east side of the house."

He wanted to order her off the ladder and back inside the house before she broke her blasted neck but he knew he had no right to do anything of the sort.

The best he could do was make sure she stayed as safe as possible.

He hated his shoulder all over again. Was he going to have to spend the rest of his life watching others do things he ought to be able to handle?

"I'll help you on one condition. When the wind hits twenty knots, you'll have to stop, whether you finish or not."

She didn't balk at the restriction as she climbed down from the ladder. "I suppose you're going to tell me now you have some kind of built-in anemometer to know what the wind speed is at all times."

He shrugged. "I've been a helicopter pilot for fifteen years and in that time I've learned a thing or two about gauging the weather. I've also learned not to mess around with Mother Nature."

"That's a lesson you learn early when you live on the coast," she answered.

She lowered the ladder and he grabbed the front end with his left hand and followed her around the corner of the house. The house's sturdy bulk sheltered them a little from the wind here but it was still cold, the air heavy and wet.

"I thought you said you kept a handyman on retainer," he said as together they propped the ladder against one corner of the porch.

She smiled. "No, you're the one who said I should. I do have a regular carpenter and he would fix all this in a second if he were around but he's been doing some work for my friend Sage's husband on one of Eben's hotels in Montana."

"Your friend's married to a hotel owner?"

He pretended ignorance while his stomach jumped as she ascended the ladder again.

"Yes. Eben Spencer owns Spencer Hotels. His company recently purchased a property here in town and that's how he met Sage."

"She's the other one who inherited Brambleberry House along with you, right?"

She nodded. "She's wonderful. You should meet her in a few weeks. She and Eben bought a house down the coast a mile or so and they come back as often as they can but they travel around quite a bit. She called me this afternoon from Patagonia, of all places!"

She started hammering again and from his vantage point, he had an entirely too clear view of that enticing expanse of skin bared at her waist when she lifted her arms. He forced himself to look away, focusing instead on the Sitka spruce dancing wildly in the wind along the road.

"Does she help you with the maintenance on the house?"

"As much as she can when she's here. And Julia helps, too. The two of us painted my living room right after Christmas."

"She's the one who lives on the second floor, right? The one with the twins."

"Right. You're going to love them. Simon will probably talk your leg off about what it's like to fly a helicopter and how you hurt your shoulder and if you carry a gun. Maddie won't have to even say a word to steal your heart in an instant. She's a doll."

His heart was a little harder to steal than that. Sometimes he wondered if he had one. And if he did, he wasn't sure a little girl would be the one to steal it.

He'd never had much to do with kids. He couldn't say he disliked them, they just always seemed like they inhabited this baffling alien world he knew little about.

"How old are the twins?" he asked.

"They turned eight a month ago. And Sage's stepdaughter Chloe is nine. When the three of them are together, there's never a dull moment. It's so wonderful."

She loved children, he realized. Before he'd gotten to know her a little these last few days, that probably would have surprised him. At first glance, she had seemed brusque and cool, not at all the sort to be patient with endless questions or sticky fingers.

But then, Anna Galvez was proving to be full of contradictions.

Just now, for instance, the crisp, buttoned-down businesswoman he had taken her for that first night looked earthy and sexy, her cheeks flushed by the cold and the exertion and her hair blown into tangles by the wind.

He wasn't interested, he reminded himself. Hadn't he spent all day reminding himself why kissing her had been a huge mistake he couldn't afford to repeat?

"There. That should do it," she said a moment later.

"Good. Now come down. That wind has picked up again."

"Gladly," she answered.

He held the ladder steady while she descended.

"Thank you," she said, her voice a little shaky until her feet were on solid ground again. "I'll admit, it helped to know you were down there giving me stability."

"No problem," he answered.

She smiled at him, her features bright and lovely and he suddenly could think of nothing but the softness of her mouth beneath his and of her seductive heat surrounding him.

They stood only a few feet apart and even though the wind lashed wildly around them and the first few drops of rain began to sting his skin, Max couldn't seem to move. He saw awareness leap into the depths of her eyes and knew instinctively she was remembering their kiss as well.

He could kiss her again. Just lean forward a little and all that heat and softness would be in his arms again...

She was the first one to break the spell between them. She drew in a deep breath and gripped the ladder and started to lower it from the porch roof while he stood gazing at her like an idiot.

"Thanks again for your help," she said, and he wondered if he imagined the tiniest hint of a quaver in her voice. "I should have done this last week. I knew a storm was on the way but I'm afraid the time slipped away from me. With an old place like Brambleberry House, there are a hundred must-do items for every one I check off."

She was talking much more than she usually did and seemed determined to avoid his gaze. She obviously didn't want a repeat of their kiss any more than he did.

Or at least any more than he *should*.

"Where does the ladder go?"

"In the garage. But I can return it."

He ignored her, just hefted it with his good arm and carried it around the house to the detached garage where Abigail had always parked her big old Oldsmobile. Conan and Anna both followed behind him.

Walking inside was like entering a time capsule of his aunt's life. It looked the same as he remembered from four years ago, with all the things Abigail had loved. Her potting table and tools, an open box of unpainted china doll faces, the tandem bicycle she had purchased several years ago.

He paused for a moment, looking around the cluttered garage and he was vaguely aware of Conan coming to stand beside him and nudging his head under Max's hand.

"It's a mess, I know. I need to clean this out as soon as I find the time. It's on my to-do list, I swear."

He said nothing, just fought down the renewed sense of loss.

"Listen," she said after a moment, "I was planning to make some pasta for dinner. I always make way too much and then feel like I have to eat it all week long, even after I'm completely sick of it. Would you like some?"

He was being sucked into Anna's life, inexorably drawn into her web. Seeing Abigail's things here only reminded him of his mission here and how he wasn't any closer to the truth than he'd been when he arrived.

"No," he said. "I'd better not."

His words sounded harsh and abrupt hanging out there alone but he didn't know how else to answer.

Her warm smile slipped away. "Another time, then."

They headed out of the garage and he was aware of Conan glaring at him.

The sky had darkened just in the few moments they had been inside the garage and it now hung heavy and gray. The scattered drops had become a light drizzle and he could see distant lightning out over the ocean.

"I should warn you we sometimes lose power in the middle of a big storm. You can find emergency candles and matches in the top drawer in the kitchen to the left of the oven."

"Thanks." They walked together up the front steps and he held the door for her to walk into the entryway.

He headed up the stairs, trying not to favor his stiff ankle, but his efforts were in vain.

"Your ankle! I completely forgot about it! I'm an idiot to make you stand out there for hours just to hold my ladder. I'm so sorry!"

"It wasn't hours and you're not an idiot. I'm fine. The ankle doesn't even hurt anymore."

It wasn't quite the truth but he wasn't about to tell her that.

He didn't want her sympathy.

He wanted something else entirely from Anna Galvez, something he damn well knew he had no business craving.

Upstairs in his apartment, Max started a fire in the grate while his TV dinner heated up in the microwave.

The wind rattled the windowpanes and sent the branches of the oak tree scraping against the glass and he tried to ignore the delicious scents wafting up from downstairs.

He could have used Conan's company. After spending the entire day with the dog, he felt oddly bereft without him.

But he supposed right now Conan was nestled on his rug in Anna's warm kitchen, having scraps of pasta and maybe a little of that yeasty bread he could smell baking.

When the microwave dinged to signal his own paltry dinner was ready, he grabbed a beer and settled into the easy chair in the living room with the remote and his dinner.

Outside, lightning flashed across the darkening sky and he told himself he should feel warm and cozy in here. But the apartment seemed silent, empty.

Just as he was about to turn on the evening news, the rocking guitar riff of "Barracuda" suddenly echoed through his apartment.

Not tonight, Mom, he thought, reaching for his cell phone and turning it off. He wasn't at all in the mood to listen to her vitriol. She would probably call all night but that didn't mean he had to listen.

Instead, he turned on the TV and divided his attention between the March Madness basketball games and the rising storm outside, doing his best to shake thoughts of the woman downstairs from his head.

He dozed off sometime in the fourth quarter of what had become a blowout.

He dreamed of dark hair and tawny skin, of deep brown eyes and a soft, delicious mouth. Of a woman in a stern blue business suit unbuttoning her jacket with agonizing slowness to reveal lush, voluptuous curves…

Max woke up with a crick in his neck to find the fire had guttered down to only a few glowing red embers. Just as she predicted, the storm must have knocked out power. The television screen was dark and the light he'd left on in the kitchen was out.

He hurried to the window and saw darkness up and down the coast. The outage was widespread, then.

From his vantage point, he suddenly saw a flashlight beam cutting across the yard below.

His instincts hummed and he peered through the sleeting rain and the wildly thrashing tree limbs to see two shapes—one human, one canine—heading across the lawn from the house to the detached garage.

What the hell was she doing out there? She'd be lucky if a tree limb didn't blow over on her.

He peered through the darkness and in her flashlight beam he saw the garage door flapping in the wind. They must not have latched it quite properly when they had returned the ladder to the garage.

Lightning lit up the yard again and he watched her wrestle the door closed then head for the house again.

He made his way carefully to his door and opened it, waiting to make sure she returned inside safely. Only silence met him from downstairs and he frowned.

What was taking her so long to come back inside?

After another moment or two, he sighed. Like it or not, he was going to have to find out.

Chapter Nine

She loved these wild coastal storms.

Anna scrambled madly back for the shelter of the porch, laughing with delight as the rain stung her cheeks and the churning wind tossed her hair around.

She wanted to lift her hands high into the air and spin around wildly in a circle in some primitive pagan dance.

She supposed most people would find that an odd reaction in a woman as careful and restrained as she tried to be in most other areas of her life. But something about the passion and intensity of a good storm sent the blood surging through her veins, made her hum with energy and excitement.

Abigail had been the same way, she remembered. Her friend used to love to sit out on the wraparound porch facing the sea, a blanket wrapped around her as she watched the storm ride across the Pacific.

Since moving to Brambleberry House nearly a year ago, Anna tried to follow the tradition as often as she could. Sort of her own way of paying tribute to Abigail and the contributions she had made to the world.

Conan shook the rain from his coat after their little foray to the garage and she laughed, grateful she hadn't removed her Gore-Tex parka yet. "Cut it out," she exclaimed. "You can do that on that side of the porch."

The dog made that snickering sound of his, then settled into the driest corner of the deep porch, closest to the house where the rain couldn't reach him.

Conan was used to these storm vigils. She would have thought the lightning and thunder would bother him but he seemed to relish them as much as she did.

Her heart still pumped from the wild run to the garage as she grabbed one of the extra blankets she had brought outside and used a corner of it to dry her face and hair from the rain.

Lightning flashed outside their protected haven and she shivered a little as she grabbed another quilt and wrapped it around her shoulders, then headed for the porch swing that had been purposely angled into a corner to shelter its occupants as much as possible from the elements.

She had barely settled in with a sigh and rattle of the swing's chains when thunder rumbled through the night.

Before it had finished, Conan was on his feet, barking with excitement.

"Settle down, bud. It's only the storm," she assured him. "And me."

She gasped at the male voice cutting through the night and quickly aimed her flashlight in the direction of it. The long roll of thunder must have muffled Max's approach. He stood several feet away, looking darkly handsome in the distant flashes of lightning.

Her heart, already racing, began to pump even faster.

This had nothing to do with the storm and everything to do with Lieutenant Maxwell.

"Is everything okay out here?" he asked, coming closer. "I saw from my window when you went out to the garage to close the door. When I didn't hear you come back inside, I was worried you might have fallen out here or something."

He was worried about her? A tiny little bubble of warmth formed in her chest but she fought down the reaction. He didn't mean anything by it. It was just simple concern of one person to another. He would have been just as conscientious if Conan had been out here in the storm.

More so, maybe. He loved her dog, while she was just the annoying landlady who wouldn't leave him alone, always inviting him to dinner and making him help her nail down loose shingles.

"I'm fine," she finally answered, unable to keep the lingering coolness from her voice after his abrupt refusal to share pasta with her earlier. "Sorry I worried you. I was just settling in to watch the storm. It's kind of a Brambleberry House tradition."

"I remember," he answered.

She gave him a quizzical look, wondering what he meant by that, though of course he couldn't see her expression in the dark.

"You remember what?" she asked.

An odd silence met her question, then he spoke quickly. "I meant, I remember doing the same thing when I visited the coast several years ago. A coastal storm is a compelling thing, isn't it?"

He felt the same tug and pull with the elements as she did? She wouldn't have expected it from the distant, contained soldier.

"It is. You're welcome to join us."

In a quick flash of lightning, she saw hesitation flicker

over those lean features—the same hesitation she had seen earlier when he had refused her invitation to dinner.

Never mind, she almost said, feeling stupid and presumptuous for even thinking he might want to sit out on a cold porch swing in the middle of a rainstorm.

But after a moment, he nodded. "Thanks. I was watching the storm from upstairs but it's not quite the same as being out here in the thick of things, is it?"

"I imagine that's a good metaphor for the life of an army helicopter pilot."

"It could very well be."

"There's room here on the swing. Or you could bring one of the rockers over from the other side of the porch, but I'm afraid they're a little damp. This is the safest corner if you want to stay out of the rain."

"Says the voice of experience, obviously."

After another odd, tense little moment of hesitation, he sat down on the swing, which swayed slightly with his weight.

The air temperature instantly increased a dozen degrees and she could smell him, spicy and male.

Lightning ripped through the night again and her blood seemed to sing with it—or maybe it was the intimacy of sitting out here with Max, broken only by the two of them wrapped in a warm cocoon of darkness while the storm raged around them.

They settled into a not uncomfortable silence, just the rain and the thunder and the occasional creak and rattle of the swing's chains.

"Are you warm enough?" she asked. "I only brought two blankets out and one is wet but I've got plenty more inside."

"I should be okay."

"Here. This one should be big enough for both of us." She pulled the blanket from around her shoulders and with a flick of her wrists, sent it billowing over both of them.

Stupid move, she realized instantly. Stupid and naive. It was one thing to sit out here with him, enjoying the storm. It was something else indeed to share a blanket while they did it. Though they weren't even touching underneath it except the occasional brush of their shoulders as they moved, it all still seemed far too intimate.

He made no move to push the blanket off, though, and she couldn't think of a way to yank it away without looking even more foolish than she already must.

"I imagine you've seen some crazy weather from the front seat of a helicopter," she said in an effort to wrench her mind from that blasted kiss the day before.

"A bit," he answered. "Sandstorms in the gulf can come up out of nowhere and you have to either play it through or set down in the middle of zero visibility."

"Scary."

"It can be. But nothing gets your heart thumping more than trying to extract a wounded soldier in poor weather conditions in the midst of possible enemy machine-gun fire."

"You love it, don't you?"

He shifted on the swing, accompanied by the rattle of creaky chains. "What?"

"Flying. What you do."

"Why do you say that?"

She shrugged. "I don't know. Your voice just sounds... different when you talk about it. More alive."

"I do love it." He paused for a long moment as the storm howled around them. "I did, anyway."

"What do you mean?"

This time, he paused so long she wasn't sure he would answer her. She had a feeling he wouldn't have if not for this illusive sense of intimacy between them, together in the darkness.

When he spoke, his voice was taut, as hard as Haystack

Rock. "The damage to my shoulder is…extensive. Between the burns and the broken bones, I've lost about seventy percent range of motion and doctors can't tell me whether I'll ever get it back. Worse than that, the infection damaged some of the nerves leading to my hand. At this point, I don't have the fine or gross motor control I need to pass the fitness test to remain a helicopter pilot in the army."

"I'm so sorry." The words sounded ridiculously lame and she wished for some other way she could comfort him.

"I'm damn lucky. I know that."

He spoke quietly, so softly she almost didn't hear him over the next rumble of thunder. "The flight medic and my copilot didn't walk away from the crash."

"Oh, Max," she murmured.

He drew in a ragged breath and then another and she couldn't help it. She reached a hand out and squeezed his fingers. He didn't seem in a hurry to release her hand and they sat together in the darkness, their fingers linked.

"What were their names?" she asked, somehow sensing the words were trapped inside him and only needed the right prompting to break free.

"Chief Warrant Officer Anthony Riani and Specialist Marybeth Shroeder. Both just kids. Marybeth had only been in country for a couple of months and Tony's wife was pregnant with their second kid. They both took the brunt of the missile hit on that side of the Black Hawk and probably died before we even went into the free fall."

She couldn't imagine what he must have seen, what he had survived. She only knew she wanted to hold him close, touched beyond measure that he would share this with her, something she instinctively sensed he didn't divulge easily.

"The crew chief and I were able to get the wounded soldier we were transporting out before the thing exploded.

We kept him stable until another Black Hawk was able to evacuate us."

"Was he okay? The soldier?"

"Oh. Yeah. He was a Humvee gunner hit by an improvised explosive device. He lost a leg but he's doing fine, home with his family in Arkansas now."

"That's good."

"Yeah. We were both at Walter Reed together for a while. He's a good man."

He finally let go of her fingers and though she knew it was silly, she suddenly felt several degrees cooler.

"I can't complain, can I?" he said. "I've still got all my pieces and even with partial function, I should eventually be able to do almost anything I want. Except fly a helicopter in the United States Army, I guess. It's looking like I'll probably have to ride a desk from now on or leave the military."

"A tough choice. What will you do?"

He sighed. "Beats me. You have any ideas? Flying helicopters is the only thing I've ever wanted to do. I never wanted to be some hotshot fighter jet pilot or anything fancy like that. Just birds. I'm not sure I can be content to sit things out on the sidelines."

"What about being a civilian pilot?"

He made a derogatory sound. "Doing traffic reports from the air or flying executives into the city who think they're too busy and important for a limousine? I don't think so."

"You could do civilian medevacs."

"I've thought about it. But to tell you the truth, I don't know that I'm capable of flying anything at this point, civilian or military. Or if I ever will be. We're in wait-and-see mode, according to the docs, which genuinely stinks when you're not a very patient person."

The storm seemed to be passing over, she thought. The lightning flashes were slowing in frequency and even the rain seemed to be easing. She didn't want this moment to end, though. She was intensely curious about this man who had survived things she couldn't even imagine.

"I'm sure you'll figure it out, Max. My friend Abigail used to say a bend in the road is not the end, unless you fail to make the turn. You just need to figure out which direction to turn. But you will."

"I'm glad one of us has a little faith."

She smiled. "You can borrow mine when you need it. Or Abigail's. She carried enough faith and goodness for all of us and I'm sure some still lingers here at Brambleberry House."

He was again silent for a long time. Then, to her shock, he reached for her hand again and held on to it as the storm continued to simmer around them. They sat for a long time like that in the darkness, while Conan snored in the corner and the storm gradually slowed its fury.

Anna's thoughts were scattered but she was aware of overriding things. She was more attracted to him than any man in her entire life. To his strength and his courage and even to his sadness.

He had been through hell and though he hadn't directly said it, she sensed he suffered great guilt over the deaths of his crew members and she wanted to ease his pain.

She was also, oddly, aware of the scent of freesia drifting over the earthy smell of wet leaves and the salty tang of the sea.

If she were Sage or Julia, she might think Abigail was making her opinion known that Harry Maxwell was a good man and she approved.

She couldn't believe Abigail was here in spirit. Abigail had been such a wonderful person that Anna couldn't believe she was anywhere but in heaven, probably doing her best to liven up things there.

But at times, even she had to admit Abigail seemed closer than at others. The smell of freesia, for instance, at just the moment she needed it. She tried to convince herself Abigail had loved the scent so much it had merely soaked into the walls of the house. But that didn't explain why it would be out here in the middle of a March rainstorm—or why she thought she caught the glitter of colorful jewels out of the corner of her gaze.

She shivered a little, refusing to give in to the urge to turn her head. Max, sitting too close beside her to miss the movement, misinterpreted it. "You're freezing. We should probably head in."

"I'm not. It's just…" She paused, feeling silly for even bringing this up but suddenly compelled to share some of Sage and Julia's theory with him. "I should probably confess something here. Something I should have told you before you rented the apartment."

He released her hand abruptly. "You're married."

She laughed, though it sounded breathless even to her. "No. Heavens, no. Not even close. Why would you even think that?"

"Not even close? Didn't you say you were engaged once?"

"Yes, years ago. I'm not close to being married right now."

"What happened to the engagement?"

She opened her mouth to tell him it was none of his business, then she closed it again. He had shared far more with her than just the painful end to an engagement that should never have happened in the first place.

"He decided he wanted a different kind of woman. Someone softer. Not so calculating. His words. At least that's what he wrote in the note he sent with his sister on the morning of what was supposed to be our wedding day."

She knew it was ridiculous but the memory still stung, even though it seemed another lifetime ago.

"Ouch."

His single, abrupt word shocked a laugh out of her. "It's been years. I rarely even think about it anymore."

"Did you love him?"

"I wouldn't have been a few hours away from marrying him if I didn't, would I?"

"Seems to me a hard, calculating woman like you wouldn't need to love a man in order to marry him. My mother never did and she's been married five times since my father died."

Now that revealed a wealth of information about his life, she thought. All of it heartbreaking.

"I'm not hard or calculating! I loved Craig. With every ounce of my twenty-four-year-old heart, I loved him. That first year afterward, I was quite certain I would literally die from the pain of the rejection. I couldn't wait to move away from my friends and family in Utah and flee to a place where no one knew me or my humiliating past."

"What's humiliating about it? Seems to me you had a lucky escape. The guy sounds like a jackass. Tell me the truth. Can you imagine now what your life would have been like if you had married him?"

She stared, stunned that he could hit right to the heart of things with the precision of a sharpshooter. "You are so right," she exclaimed. "I would have been completely miserable. I was just too young and stupid to realize it at the time."

It was a marvelously liberating discovery. She supposed she had known it, somewhere deep inside, but for so long she had held on to her mortification and the shame of being jilted on her wedding day. Somehow in the process, she had lost all perspective.

That day had seemed such a defining moment in her life, only because she had allowed it be, she realized.

She had become fearful about trusting anyone and had

learned to erect careful defenses to keep people safely on the perimeter of her life. She had focused on her career, on first making By-the-Wind successful as Abigail's manager, then on building the company after she purchased it from her and then adding the second store to further cement her business plan.

Though she didn't think she had completely become what Craig called her—hard, calculating, driven—she had certainly convinced herself her strengths lay in business, not in personal relationships.

Maybe she was wrong about that.

"So if you're not married, what's your big secret?"

She blinked at Max, too busy with her epiphany to follow the trail of conversation. "Sorry. What?"

"You said you had some dark confession to make that you should have told me before I rented the apartment."

"I never said dark. Did I say dark?"

"I don't remember. I'm sure it was."

"No. It's not. It's just…well, rather silly."

"I could use more silly in my life right now."

She smiled and nudged his shoulder with hers. "All right. What's your opinion on the paranormal?"

"I'm not sure I know how to answer that. Are we talking alien visitations or bloodsucking vampires?"

"Neither. I'm talking about ghosts. Or I guess ghost, singular. As in the ghost that some residents of Brambleberry House believe shares the house with us. My friend Abigail."

"You're saying you think Abigail still walks the halls of Brambleberry House."

"I didn't say *I* believed it. But Sage and Julia do. They won't listen to reason. They're absolutely convinced she's still here and that Conan is her familiar, I guess you could say. She works through him to weave her Machiavellian plans. Though I don't really know if one should use that word when all her plans seem to be more on the benevolent side."

The rain had slowed and a corner of the moon peeked out from behind some of the clouds, lending enough light to the scene that she could clearly see his astonished expression.

He stared at her for an endless moment, until she was quite certain he must believe her barking mad, then his head rocked back on his neck and he began to laugh, his shoulders shaking so much the swing rocked crazily on its chains and Conan padded over to investigate.

She had never seen Max so lighthearted. He looked years younger, his features relaxed and almost happy. She could only gaze at him, entranced by this side of him.

The entire evening, she had been trying to ignore how attracted she was to him. But right now, while laughter rippled out of him and his eyes were bright with humor, the attraction blossomed to a hot, urgent hunger.

She had to touch him. Just for a moment, she told herself, then she would go back inside the house and do her best to rebuild her defenses against this man who had survived horrors she couldn't imagine but who could still find humor at the idea of a ghost and her dog.

Her heart clicked just like the rain on the shingles she had just fixed as she drew in a sharp breath, then leaned forward and brushed her mouth against his.

Chapter Ten

Her mouth was warm and soft and tasted like cinnamon candy.

For all of maybe three seconds, he couldn't seem to move past the shock of it, completely frozen by the unexpectedness of the kiss and by the instant heat that crashed against him like those waves against the headland.

He forgot all about his amusement at the idea of his aunt Abigail using a big, gangly dog to work her schemes from the afterlife. He forgot the rain and the wind and the vow he had made to himself not to kiss her again.

He forgot everything but the sheer wonder of Anna in his arms again, of those soft curves beside him, of her scent, sweet and feminine, that had been slowly driving him insane all evening long as she sat beside him, tugging at him until his senses were filled with nothing but her.

Her arms twisted around his neck and he deepened the

kiss, breathing deeply of that enticing, womanly scent and pulling her closer until she was nearly on his lap.

For the first time since he had sat down on the porch swing next to her, he was grateful for the blanket around them. Now it was no longer a curse, lending an intimacy he didn't want. Instead, the blanket had become a warm, close shelter from the cold air outside, drawing them closer.

Nothing else existed here but the two of them and the wild need glittering between them.

Kissing her again had a sense of inevitability to it, as if all day he had been waiting for only this. Suspended in a state of hungry anticipation to once again feel her hands in his hair, her soft curves pressed against him, the rapid beat of his heart.

Since the first time he kissed her, his body had been aching to have her in his arms again. That's why he had punished his ankle with a long walk on the shore, why he had spent the morning at the gym he'd found in Seaside working on his physical therapy exercises, why he had done his best to stay away from Brambleberry House all day.

Now that he had rediscovered the wonder of a woman's touch—*this* woman's touch—he couldn't manage to think about anything else. And even when he wasn't consciously thinking about it, his subconscious had been busy remembering.

This was better than anything he might have dreamed. She was warm and responsive, her mouth eager against his.

It was an intense and erotic kiss, just the two of them alone in the night in this warm shelter while the storm battered the coast around them, and he wanted it to go on forever.

Still, he had a vague awareness even as their bodies heated that the storm was calming—or at least moving farther inland, leaving them behind. The lightning strikes became more infrequent, the rolling thunder more distant.

He didn't care. Nothing else mattered but having her in his arms, slaking this raging thirst for her.

She moved a little, her soft curves brushing against his sling, but she quickly drew back.

"Sorry," she exclaimed.

"You don't have to be careful. I'm sorry my arm is in the way."

"It's not. I'm just afraid of hurting you."

"Let me worry about that."

"Are you? Worried about it, I mean?"

"What red-blooded male in his right mind would worry about a stupid thing like a cast on his arm right now?" he murmured against her mouth.

Her low laugh sent chills rippling down his spine.

"Do that again," he said.

In the darkness, she blinked at him. "Do…what?"

"Laugh like that. I would have to say, Ms. Galvez, that was just about the sexiest sound I've ever heard."

"You're crazy," she said, though she gave a self-conscious laugh when she said it and he thought he just might be content to sit there all night letting his imagination travel all sorts of wicked roads inspired by the sound.

"I must be. That's what six months in an army hospital will get you."

"I'm so sorry you had to go through that," she whispered. "I wish I could make everything okay."

To his shock, she planted a barely there kiss on the corner of his mouth then one on the other side. It was a stunningly sweet gesture and he felt something hard and tight that had been inside him for a long time suddenly break loose.

Had anyone ever shown such gentle compassion to him? He sure as hell couldn't remember it. To his dismay, tears burned behind his eyelids and he wanted to lean into her and just lose himself in her touch.

A fragile tenderness wrapped around them like Aunt Abigail's morning glory vines. He pulled her more firmly on his lap, solving the quandary of his cast by lifting the whole thing out of the way and resting his arm against her back as she nestled against his chest.

They kissed and touched for a long time, until he was aching with need, until she was shivering.

"Are you cold?"

Her laugh was rough. "Not even close."

Still, even as she said the words, she let out a long breath and he sensed her withdrawal, though she didn't physically pull out of his arms.

"This is crazy, Max. What are we doing here? This isn't…I don't do this kind of thing. I…we barely know each other."

He was having a hard time making his addled brain think at all but the still-functioning corner of his mind knew she was absolutely right. He had only been here a few days and in that time, he had been anything but honest with her.

But he didn't agree when she said she barely knew him. Right now, he felt as if she knew him better than anyone else alive. He had told her things he hadn't been able to share with the shrinks at Walter Reed.

"I don't know what this thing is between us but I'm fiercely attracted to you."

She let out a shaky breath and pulled out of his arms with a breathless little laugh. "Okay. Good to know."

"But then, you probably figured that out already."

"I believe I did, Lieutenant. And, uh, right back at you. So what do we do about it?"

He had a number of suggestions, none of which he was willing to share with her.

Before he could answer at all, the porch was suddenly flooded with lights as the electricity flashed back on.

Her eyes looked wide and shocked and she slid away from him on the porch swing as Conan gave a resigned-sounding sigh.

"Is that some kind of message?" Max asked with a rueful laugh. "Maybe the ghost of Brambleberry House is subtly telling us it's time to go inside."

"Ha. Doubtful. If I bought in to Sage and Julia's theory, Abigail's ghost would more likely be the one who cut the power in the first place," she muttered.

"You didn't tell me they had a theory about the ghost. I just figured she maybe wanted to hang around and make sure you treated her house the way she wanted."

He couldn't quite imagine Abigail as a malicious poltergeist. Not that she didn't love a little mischief and mayhem, but she wouldn't have caused it at any inconvenience or expense to someone else.

Though he might have expected things to be awkward with the heat and passion that still sparkled between them, he felt surprisingly comfortable with Anna.

He enjoyed her company, he realized. Whether they were talking or kissing or sitting quietly, he found being with her soothing, as if she settled some restless spirit inside him in a way nothing else ever had.

"Abigail was always a bit of a romantic," Anna answered. "She would have enjoyed setting the scene like this. The rain, the storm. All of it."

While he was trying to picture his aunt working behind the scenes as some great manipulator, Conan ambled off the porch steps and out in the misting rain.

"You don't really think some…ghost had anything to do with what just happened, do you?"

"I'm afraid my feet are planted too firmly on the ground for me to buy in to the whole thing like Sage and Julia do. And besides, while I firmly believe Abigail could have done anything she set her mind to, cutting off power along the entire coast so the two of us could…" Her voice trailed off and he was intrigued to see color soak those high, elegant cheekbones. "Could make out is probably a little beyond her capabilities."

Just as she finished speaking, the porch lights flickered off for maybe two seconds before they flashed back on again.

When they did, her eyes were bright with laughter.

"I wish you could see your face right now," she exclaimed.

He scanned the porch warily. "I'm just trying to figure out if some octogenarian ghost is going to come walking through the walls of the house any minute now with a bottle of wine and a dozen roses."

She laughed. "I don't believe you have anything to worry about. I've never seen her and I don't expect to."

Her smile faded and her dark eyes looked suddenly wistful, edged with sadness. "I wish Abigail *would* walk through that wall, though. I wish you could have known her. I think you would have loved her. She was…amazing. That's the only word for it. Amazing. She drew everyone to her in that way that very few people in the world have. The kind of person who just makes people around her feel happy and important, whether they're billionaire hotel owners or struggling college students."

"She must have been a good friend."

"More than that. I can't explain it, really. I just think you would have loved her. And I *know* she would have adored you."

"Me? Why do you say that?"

"She was always a sucker for a man in uniform. She was engaged to marry a man who died in Korea. He was her one true love and she never really got over him."

He stared. "I never…" Knew that, he almost said, but caught himself just in time. "How do you know that?"

"She told me about him once and then she never wanted to talk about him again," Anna answered. "She said he was the other half of her heart and the best person she'd ever known and she had mourned his loss every single day of her life."

Why had Abigail never told him anything about a lost love? He supposed it might not be the thing one confided in a young boy. What bothered him more was that he had never once thought to ask. He had always assumed she loved her independent life, loved being able to come and go as she pleased without having to answer to anyone else.

He found it terribly sad to think about her living in this big house all these years, mourning a love taken from her too soon.

"I would think a heartbreak like that would have given her an aversion to military men."

Anna shook her head, her eyes soft. "It didn't. I know she had a nephew in the military. I don't even know what branch but she was always so proud of him."

"Oh?"

"Her Jamie. I never met him. He didn't visit her much but she was still crazy about him. Abigail was like that. She loved wholeheartedly, no matter what."

Her words were a harsh condemnation, and the hell of it was, he couldn't even defend himself. He might not have visited Abigail as often as he would have liked, but it wasn't as if he had abandoned her.

They had stayed in touch over the years, he just hadn't been as conscientious about it while he was deployed.

"She sounds like a real character," he said, his voice gruff.

She flashed him a searching look and opened her mouth but before she could speak, Conan bounded back up the porch steps and shook out his wet coat on both of them.

Max managed to pull the blanket up barely in time to protect their faces.

"Conan!" she exclaimed. "Cut that out!"

The dog made that snickering sound he seemed to have perfected, then sauntered back to the corner.

"If you're looking for a signal to go inside, I believe that's a little more concrete than some ghostly manifestation."

"You're probably right," he said, reluctance in his voice.

"You're welcome to stay out here longer. I can leave the lantern and the blankets."

"I'd rather have you."

The words slipped out and hovered between them. "Sorry. I shouldn't have said that. Forget it."

She blinked. "No, I—I…"

She looked so adorably befuddled in the glow from the porch light—and just so damn beautiful with that thick, glossy dark hair and that luscious mouth—that he couldn't help himself.

One more kiss. That's all, he promised himself as he pulled her closer.

She sighed his name and leaned into him. She was small and curvy and delicious and he couldn't seem to get enough.

He touched the warm, enticing skin above the waistband of her jeans. She gave a little shuddering breath and he felt her stomach muscles contract sharply. Her mouth tangled with his and she made a tiny sound of arousal that shot straight to his gut.

He feathered his fingers along her skin, then danced across it until he met an enticing scrap of lace. He curved his thumb over her and felt her nipple harden. She arched into him and a white haze of hunger gnawed at him, until all he could think about was touching her, tasting her.

She gasped his name.

"I need to stop or I'm afraid I won't be able to."

"To what?"

He gave a raw laugh and kissed her mouth one last time then leaned his forehead against hers, feeling as breathless as if he were a new recruit forced to do a hundred push-ups in front of the entire unit.

He wanted to take things further. God knew, he wanted to. But he knew it would be a huge mistake.

"To stop. I don't want to but I'm afraid what seems like a brilliant idea right now out here will take on an entirely different perspective in the cold light of morning."

After a long moment, she sighed. "You're probably right."

She rose from the porch swing first and though it was one of the toughest things he had ever asked of himself, he helped her gather the blankets and carry them inside the foyer.

"Good night, Anna," he said at her apartment door. "I enjoyed the storm."

"Which one?" she asked with a surprisingly impish smile.

He shook his head but decided he would be wise not to answer.

His last sight as he headed up the stairs to his apartment was of Conan sitting by Anna's doorway looking up at him, and he could swear the dog was shaking his head in disgust.

His TV had switched back on when the power returned and some Portland TV weatherman was rambling on about the storm that was just beginning to sweep through town.

He turned off the noise then went to the windows, watching the moonlight as it peeked between clouds to dance across the water.

What the hell was he going to do now?

Anna Galvez was no more a scam artist than his aunt Abigail.

He didn't know about Sage Benedetto but since he had

come to trust Abigail's judgment about Anna, he figured he should probably trust it with Sage as well.

Anna had loved his aunt. He had heard the vast, unfeigned affection in her voice when she had talked about her, when she had told him how she wished he could have known Abigail.

She loved Abigail and missed her deeply, he realized. Maybe even as much as he did.

He would have to tell her the truth—that he was Abigail's nephew and had concealed his identity so he could basically spy on her.

After the heated embrace they had just shared, how was he supposed to come clean and tell her he had been lying to her for days?

It sounded so ugly and sordid just hanging out there like that, but he knew he was going to have to figure out a way.

As was often the case after a wild coastal storm, the morning dawned bright and cloudless and gorgeous.

Anna awoke in her bed in an odd, expectant mood. She rarely slept with the curtains pulled, so that she could look out at the sea first thing in the morning. Today, the waves were pale pink frothed with white.

Conan must have slept in. He was usually in here first thing in the morning, begging for his run, but she supposed the late-night stormwatching had tired him out.

She wished she could say the same. She had tossed and turned half the night, her body restless and aching.

She sighed and rolled over onto her back. She was *still* restless and achy and she was very much afraid Harry Maxwell had ruined stormwatching for her for the rest of her days. How could she ever sit out on the porch watching the waves whip across the sky without remembering the heat and magic of his arms?

FREE BOOKS OFFER

To get you started, we'll send you
2 FREE books and a FREE gift

There's no catch, everything is **FREE**

Accepting your 2 **FREE** books and **FREE** mystery gift
places you under no obligation to buy anything.

Be part of the Mills & Boon® Book Club™ and receive your favourite
Series books up to 2 months before they are in the shops and delivered
straight to your door. Plus, enjoy a wide range of **EXCLUSIVE** benefits!

- Best new women's fiction – delivered right to
  your door with FREE P&P

- Avoid disappointment – get your books up to
  2 months before they are in the shops

- No contract – no obligation to buy

We hope that after receiving your free books you'll
want to remain a member. But the choice is yours.
So why not give us a go? You'll be glad you did!

Visit **millsandboon.co.uk** to stay up to date
with offers and to sign-up for our newsletter

2 **FREE** books
and a
FREE gift

E9EI

Mrs/Miss/Ms/Mr _____ Initials _____

BLOCK CAPITALS PLEASE

Surname _____

Address _____

_____

Postcode _____

Email _____

MILLS & BOON®
Pure reading pleasure

NO STAMP
NEEDED!

MILLS & BOON®
Book Club

FREE BOOK OFFER
FREEPOST CN81
CROYDON
CR9 3WZ

NO STAMP
NECESSARY
IF POSTED IN
THE U.K. OR N.I.

Blast him, anyway.

She sighed. No. It wasn't his fault. She had known she was tempting fate when she kissed him but she hadn't been able to control herself.

She wanted a wild, passionate fling with Harry Maxwell.

She drew in a shaky breath. How was that for a little blunt truth first thing in the morning?

She was fiercely attracted to the man. More attracted than she had ever been in her life. She wanted him, even though she knew he would be leaving soon. Maybe *because* she knew he would be leaving soon.

For once in her life, she didn't want to fret or rehash the past. She wanted to live in the heady urgency of the moment.

She blew out a breath. Even if she ever dared tell them— which she wouldn't—Sage and Julia would never believe she was lying here in her bed contemplating such a thing with a man she had only known for a matter of days.

How, exactly, did one go about embarking on a fling? She had absolutely no idea.

She supposed she could take the direct route and go upstairs dressed in a flimsy negligee. But first she would have to actually go out and *buy* a flimsy negligee. And then, of course, she would have to somehow find the courage to put it on, forget about actually having the guts to walk upstairs in it.

She sighed. Okay, she didn't know exactly how she could work the logistics of the thing.

"But I *will* figure it out," she said aloud.

Conan suddenly barked from the doorway and she felt foolish for talking to herself, even if her only witness was her dog, who didn't seem to mind at all when she held long conversations with herself through him.

"Thanks for the extra half hour," she said to the dog.

He grinned as if to say *you're welcome,* then headed to

the door to stand as an impatient sentinel, as was his morning ritual. She knew from long experience that he would stay there until she surrendered to the inevitable and got dressed to walk him down the beach.

This morning she didn't make him wait long. She hurried into jeans and a sweatshirt then pulled her hair back into a ponytail and grabbed her parka against the still-cold March mornings.

Conan danced on the end of his leash as she opened the door to Brambleberry House, then even he seemed to stop in consternation.

The yard was a mess. The storm must have wreaked more havoc than she'd realized from her spot on the seaward side of the house. The lawn was covered with storm debris—loose shingles and twigs and several larger branches that must have fallen in the night since she was certain she would have heard them crack even from the other side of the house.

Okay, she was going to have to put her tentative seduction plans for Harry Maxwell on the back burner. First thing after walking Conan, she was going to have to deal with this mess.

Chapter Eleven

She cut Conan's walk short, taking him north only as far as Haystack Rock before turning back to head down toward home and all the work waiting for her there.

At least it was an off-season Sunday, when her schedule was more flexible. As a small-business owner, she always felt as if she had one more thing she should be doing. But one of the most important things Abigail had taught her was to be protective of her time off.

You've got to allow yourself to be more than just the store, Abigail had warned her in the early days after she purchased By-the-Wind. *Don't put all the eggs of yourself into the basket of work or you're only going to end up a scrambled mess.*

It wasn't always possible to take time off during the busier summer season, but during the slower spring and winter months she tried to keep Sundays to herself to recharge for the week ahead.

Of course, cleaning up storm debris wasn't exactly relaxing and invigorating, but it was better than sitting in her office with a day full of paperwork.

Her mind was busy with all that she had to do as she walked up the sand dunes toward the house. She let Conan off his leash as soon as she closed the gate behind her and he immediately raced around the corner of the house. She followed him, curious at his urgency, and was stunned to find Max wearing a work glove on his uninjured hand and pushing a wheelbarrow already piled high with fallen limbs.

Her heart picked up a pace at the sight of him greeting Conan with an affectionate pat and she thought how gorgeous he looked in the warm glow of morning, lean and lithe and masculine.

"Hey, you don't have to do that," she called. "You're a renter, not the hired help."

He looked up from Conan. "Do you have a chain saw?" he asked, ignoring her admonition. "Some of these limbs are a little too big to cart off very easily."

"Abigail had a chain saw. It's in the garage. I'm not sure when it was used last, though, so it's probably pretty dull."

She hesitated, trying to couch her words in a way to cause the least assault to his pride. "Um, I hate to bring this up but don't you think your shoulder might make running a chain saw a little tough?"

He looked down at the sling with frustration flickering in his eyes, as if he had forgotten his injury.

"Actually, she also had a wood chipper," she added quickly. "I was planning to just chip most of this to use as mulch in the garden in a few weeks' time. The machine is pretty complicated, though, and it's a two-person job. To tell you the truth, I could use some help."

"Of course," he answered promptly.

She smiled, lost for just a moment in the memory of all they had shared on the porch swing the night before.

She might have stood staring at him all morning if Conan hadn't nudged her, as if to remind her she had work to do.

"Let me just find my gloves and then we can get to work."

"No problem. There's plenty out here to keep me busy."

She hurried inside the house and headed for the hall tree, where she kept her extra gardening gloves and the muck boots she wore when she worked out in the garden.

The man had no right to look so gorgeous first thing in the morning when she could see in the hall mirror that she looked bedraggled and windblown from walking along the seashore.

The idea of a casual fling had seemed so enticing this morning when she had been lying in bed. When she was confronted with six feet of sexy male in a denim workshirt and leather gloves, she wondered what on earth she had been thinking.

She had a very strong feeling that a casual fling with a man like Lieutenant Maxwell would turn out to be anything but casual.

Not that a fling with him seemed likely anytime in the near future. He had seemed like a polite stranger this morning, in vivid contrast to the heat between them the night before.

She sighed. It was a nice fantasy while it lasted and certainly helped take her mind off Grayson Fletcher and the misery of the trial, which would be resuming all too soon.

When she returned to the yard, she couldn't see Max anywhere. But since Conan was sprawled out at the entrance to the garage, she had a fairly solid idea where to find him.

Inside, she found him trying to extricate the chipper, which was wedged tightly behind an old mattress frame and a pile of two-by-fours Will had brought over to use on various repairs around the house.

The chipper had wheels for rolling across the lawn but it was still bulky and unwieldy. She stepped forward to give him a hand clearing a path. "I know, this garage is a mess. With every project we do on the house, we seem to be collecting more and more stuff and now we're running out of places to put it all."

"You'll have to build a garage annex for it all."

She smiled. "Right. A garage for the garage. Sage would love the idea. To tell you the truth, I don't know what else to do. I hate to throw anything away. I'm so afraid we'll toss an old lamp or something and then find out it was Abigail's favorite or some priceless antique that had been in her family for generations."

"You can't keep the house like a museum for her."

"I know. She wouldn't want that and what little family she had doesn't seem to care much about maintaining their heritage. But I still worry. My parents brought very little with them from Mexico when they came across the border. Their families were both poor and didn't have much for them to bring but sometimes I wish I had more old things that told the story of my ancestors and what their lives might have been like."

An odd expression crossed his features and he opened his mouth to answer but before he could, she pulled the last obstacle out of the way so they could pull out the chipper.

"Here we go. That should give us a clear path."

They pulled the chipper out of the chaotic garage and into the sunshine while Conan watched them curiously.

"Any idea how to work this thing?" Max asked.

She smiled. "A year ago, my answer to that question would have been a resounding no, but I've had to learn a few things since I've been at Brambleberry House. This home ownership thing is not for the weak or timid, I'll tell you that much. I've become an expert at removing wallpaper, puttying walls, even wielding a toilet snake. This chipper business is easy compared to that."

For the next two hours, they worked together cleaning up the yard while Conan lazed in whatever dappled bit of sunbeam he could find. It was a gorgeous, sunny early spring day, the kind she always considered a gift from above here in Oregon.

When the fallen branches were cleared and the beautiful wood chips from them stored at the side of the garage for a few more weeks until she had time to prepare the flower beds, Max helped her gather up the loose shingles and replace the gutter that had blown down.

"Anything else we can do?" he asked when they finished and were sitting together on the porch steps taking a breather.

"I don't think so. Not right now, anyway. It's an endless job, this home maintenance thing."

"But not a bad way to spend a beautiful morning."

She smiled, enjoying his company immensely. Even with only one good hand, he worked far harder than most men she knew. He carried heavy limbs under one arm and though he quickly figured out he couldn't push the wheelbarrow with one hand without toppling it over, he ended up dragging out Abigail's old garden wagon and pulling the limbs and wood chips in that.

"I used to hate gardening when I was a kid," she told him. "My parents always had a huge vegetable garden. We would grow peppers and green beans and sweet corn and of course we kids always had to do the weeding. I vowed I was going to live in a condominium the rest of my life where I wouldn't have to get out at the crack of dawn to pick beans."

"But here you are." He gestured to the house.

"Here I am. And you know something weird? Taking care of the garden and yard has become my favorite part of living here. I can't wait until the flowers start coming out in a few weeks. You will be astonished at Abigail's garden. It's a magic place."

He made a noncommittal sound, as if he wasn't quite convinced, and she smiled. "I guess you don't have much opportunity for gardening, living in base housing as you said you've done."

"Not in the army, no," he said in what she had come to think of as his cautious voice. "Various places I've stayed, I've had the chance to do a little but not much."

"You can do all you want at Brambleberry House while you're here. All hands are welcome in Abigail's garden, experienced or not."

"I'll keep that in mind."

Conan brought over a sturdy twig they must have missed and dropped it at his feet. Max obliged him by picking it up and tossing left-handed for the dog to scamper after.

It was a lovely moment and Anna found she didn't want it to end. "Do you feel like a drive?" she asked suddenly.

"With a specific destination involved or just for the ride?"

"A little of both. I need to head down to Lincoln City to drop off some items that were delivered by mistake to the store up here. I'd love some company. I'll even take you to lunch at my favorite restaurant at Neskowin Beach on the way down. My way of paying you back for your help today."

"You don't owe me anything for that. I didn't do much."

She could have argued with him but she decided she wasn't in the mood to debate. "The offer's still open."

He shifted on the step and looked up at the blue sky for a long moment and then turned back at her with a rather wary smile. "It *is* a gorgeous day for a drive."

She returned his smile, then laughed when Conan gave two sharp barks, whether from anticipation or just plain excitement, she couldn't guess. "Wonderful. Can you give me about half an hour to clean up?"

"Only half an hour?"

She grinned at him as she climbed to her feet. "Lieutenant, I grew up with three brothers in a little house with only one bathroom. A girl learns to work her magic fast under those circumstances."

She was rewarded with a genuine smile, one that warmed her clear to her toes. She hurried through her shower and dressed quickly. And though she would have liked to spend some time blow-drying her hair and fixing it into something long and luxurious and irresistible, she had to be satisfied with pulling it into a simple style, held away from her face with a yellow bandeau that matched her light sweater.

She did take time to apply a light coat of makeup, though even that was more than she usually bothered with.

"It's not a date," she assured Conan, who sat watching her with curious eyes as she applied eyeliner and mascara.

This is not a date and I am not breathless, she told herself when the doorbell rang a few moments later.

She answered the door and knew that last one was a blatant lie. She felt as if she were standing on the bluffs above Heceta Head with the wind hitting her from every side.

He wore Levi's and a brushed-cotton shirt in a color that matched the dark spruce outside. Hunger and anticipation curled through her insides.

"Do you need more time?" he asked.

"Not at all. I only have to grab my purse. Oh, and Conan's leash. Are you okay with him coming along? He pouts if I leave him alone too long."

"I expected it."

That was one of the things she appreciated most about him—his wholehearted acceptance of her dog.

Conan raced ahead as they headed out to her minivan and waited until she opened the door. His customary spot was in the passenger seat but he seemed content to sprawl

out in the cargo area this trip, along with the boxes she had
carefully strapped down the day before.

She backed with caution out of the driveway and waited
until they were on the road heading south before she spoke.
"I know you've been at least as far south as Neah-Kah-Nie
Mountain. Have you gone farther down the coast?"

"Not this trip," he answered. "It's been several years."

"I've been driving to Lincoln City two or three times a
week for nine months and I still never get tired of it."

"Is that how long you've had the store there?"

She nodded, then fell silent, remembering her starry
dreams of last summer, when she had first opened the
second store. She had wanted so desperately for the store
to succeed and had imagined opening a third and maybe
even a fourth store someday, until everywhere on the coast,
people would think of By-the-Wind when they thought of
books and unique gift items.

Now her dreams were in tatters and most days when she
drove this road, she arrived with tight shoulder muscles and
her stomach in knots.

"Did I say something wrong?" Max asked, and she
realized she had been silent for a good mile or more.

"No. It's not you. It's just…"

She hesitated to tell him, though the trial was certainly
common knowledge.

No doubt he would hear about it sooner or later and it was
probably better that she give him the information herself.

Her hands tightened on the steering wheel. "My professional life is a mess," she admitted. "Once in a while I'm
able to forget about it for an hour or so at a time but then
it all comes creeping back."

She was almost afraid to look at him to gauge his
reaction but she finally dared a quick look and found his
expression unreadable. "Want to talk about it?"

"I don't want to ruin your enjoyment of the spectacular coastal scenery with such a long, boring, sordid story."

"Can a story be boring and sordid at the same time?"

The tongue-in-cheek question surprised a laugh from her when she least expected to find much of anything amusing. "Good point."

And a good reminder that she shouldn't take herself so seriously. She hadn't lost any team members to enemy fire. She hadn't been shot down over hostile territory or suffered severe burns or spent months in the hospital.

This was a tough hurdle and professionally and personally humiliating for her but it wasn't the end of the world.

She didn't know where to start and she didn't want to look like an idiot to him. But he had been brutally honest with her the night before and she suddenly found she wanted to share this with Max.

"I trusted the wrong person," she finally said. "I guess the story all starts with that."

Could the woman make him feel any more guilty, however unwittingly?

As Max listened to Anna's story of fraud and betrayal by the former store manager of her Lincoln City store, shame coalesced in his gut.

She talked about how she had been lied to for months, how she had ignored warning signs and hadn't trusted her gut.

How was Max going to tell her he had lied about his identity?

He had a strong suspicion her past experience with this charlatan wasn't going to make her the forgiving sort when he came clean.

"So here we are six months later," she finally said. "Everything is such a disaster. My business is in shambles, I've got suppliers coming out of the woodwork with invoices I thought had been paid months ago and worse, at least two dozen of my customers had their credit and debit cards used fraudulently. It's been a months-long nightmare and I have no idea when I'll ever be able to wake up."

Max remembered his speculation when he read the sketchy information online about the trial that maybe she had been involved in the fraud, a partner who was letting her manager take the fall while she reaped the benefits.

The thought of that now was laughable and he was sorry he had even entertained the idea. She sounded sick about the trial, about the fraud, especially about her customers who had suffered.

"You said this Fletcher jerk has been charged?"

"Oh, yes. That's part of the joy of this whole thing, out there in the public eye for everyone to see what an idiot I've been."

"It's not your fault the guy was a scumbag thief."

"No. But it is my fault I hired the scumbag thief to mind my store and gave him access to the personal information of all my customers and vendors who trusted me to protect that. It's my fault I didn't supervise things as closely as I should have, which allowed him more room and freedom to stick his fingers in as many pies as he could find."

"That's a lot of weight for you to bear."

"My name is the one on the business license. It's my responsibility."

"When will the trial wrap up?"

"This week, I think. Closing arguments start tomorrow and I'm hoping for a quick verdict soon after that. I'll just be so glad when it's over."

"That bad?"

She shrugged and tried to downplay it but he saw the truth in her eyes. "Every day when I walk in the courtroom,

I feel like they ought to hand me a dunce cap and a sign to hang around my neck—World's Biggest Idiot."

"You've sat through the entire trial?"

"Every minute of it. Grayson Fletcher stole from me, he stole from customers, he stole from my vendors. He took my reputation and I want to make sure he pays for it."

He had seen seasoned war veterans who didn't have the kind of grit she possessed in order to walk into that court-room each day. He was astonished at the soft tenderness seeping through him, at his fierce desire to take her hand and assure her everything would be okay.

He couldn't do it. Not with his own deception lying between them.

"Anna, I need to tell you something," he said.

"What?" For just an instant, she shifted her gaze from the road, her eyes wary and watchful.

"I haven't been…" Honest, he started to say, but before the words were out, Conan suddenly interrupted him with a terrible retching sound like he had a tennis ball lodged in his throat.

Until this moment, the dog had been lying peacefully in the cargo area of the minivan but now he poked his head between the driver and passenger seats, retching and gagging dramatically.

"Conan!" she exclaimed. "What's going on, bud? You okay?"

The dog continued making those horrible noises and Anna swerved off the road to the wide shoulder, turned off the van and hurried to the side to open the sliding door.

Conan clambered out and walked back and forth a few times on his leash. He gagged once or twice more, then seemed to take care of whatever had been bothering him.

A moment later, with what seemed like remarkable non-chalance, he headed to a clump of grass and lifted his leg, then wandered back to the two of them, planted his haunches in the grass and looked at them expectantly.

Anna watched him, a frown on her lovely features. "Weird. What was that all about?"

"Carsick, maybe?" Max suggested.

"Conan's never carsick," she answered. "I swear, he has the constitution of a horse."

"Maybe he just needed a little fresh air and a convenient fern."

"So why the theatrics? Maybe he just needed attention. Behave yourself," she ordered the dog as she let him back into the back of the vehicle.

Conan grinned at both of them and Max could have sworn the dog winked at him, though of course he knew that was crazy.

"We're almost to Neskowin and my favorite place," Anna said as she returned to the driver's seat. "Are you ready for lunch?"

He still needed to tell her he was Abigail's nephew. But somehow the time didn't seem right now.

"Sure," he answered. "I'm starving."

"Trust me, you're going to love this place. Wait until you try the chili shrimp."

He couldn't remember the last time he had permitted himself to genuinely relax and have fun.

In the military, he had been completely focused on his career, on becoming the best Black Hawk pilot in his entire division. And then the last six months had been devoted to healing—first the burns and the fractures, then the infection, then the nerve damage.

All that seemed a world away from this gorgeous stretch of coastline and Anna.

While they savored fresh clam chowder and crab legs

at a charming restaurant with a spectacular view, they watched the waves roll in and gulls wheel overhead as they laughed and talked.

She told him about growing up with three older brothers in Utah and the trouble they would get in. She told him about her father dying in an industrial accident and her mother's death a few years later from cancer.

She talked about her brother the biologist who lived in Costa Rica with his wife and their twin toddler girls, who knew more Spanish than they did English and could swim like little guppies. About her brother Daniel, a sheriff back home in Utah and his wife, Lauren, who was the only physician for miles around their small town and about her brother Marc, whose wife had just left him to raise their two little boys on his own.

He would have been content just to listen to her talk about her family with her hands gesturing wildly and her face more animated than he had seen it. But she seemed to expect some conversation in return.

Since he didn't think she'd be interested in the stepsiblings he had barely known even when his mother had been married to their respective fathers, he told her instead about his real family. About his army unit and learning to fly his bird, about night sorties when it was pitch-black beneath him as they flew over villages with no electricity and he felt like he was flying over some lunar landscape, about the strength and courage of the people he had met there.

After lunch, they took a short walk with Conan along the quiet, cold beach before continuing the short trip to Lincoln City.

Though he had been careful not to touch her all day, he was aware of the heat simmering between them. He would have to be dead to miss it—the kick of his heartbeat when she smiled, the tightening of his insides when she laughed and ran after Conan on the beach, the burning ache he fought down all day to kiss her once again.

She was the most beautiful woman he had ever known but he couldn't find any words to tell her so that didn't sound corny and artificial. As they reached the busy outskirts of Lincoln City, he watched, fascinated, as his light-hearted companion seemed to become more focused and reserved with each passing mile.

By the time they drove into a small district of charming storefronts and upscale restaurants and pulled up in front of the cedar-and-brick facade that said By-the-Wind Two, she seemed a different person.

"You can wait here if you'd like," she said after she had turned off the engine.

"I'd like to see your store, if that's okay with you," he said. There was a much smaller likelihood of anyone recognizing him as Abigail's nephew in Lincoln City than if he'd gone into the original By-the-Wind, he figured. Beyond that, he really did want to see where she worked.

"Can I carry something for you?" he asked.

"I've got six boxes here. They're extremely fragile so we would probably be better off making a few trips rather than trying to haul everything in at once," she said.

He picked up a box with his good arm and followed her to a side entrance to the store, which she unlocked and propped open for them. They carried the boxes into what looked like a back storage room then they made two more trips each, the last one accompanied by Conan.

After they set down the last boxes, Anna led the way into the main section of the store.

He looked around with curiosity and found the shop comfortable and welcoming, very much in the same vein as Aunt Abigail's Cannon Beach store. Something jazzy and

light played on a hidden stereo system and the wall sconce
lighting in the bookstore area made all the books seem mysterious and enticing. Plump chairs invited patrons to stay
and relax and apparently they did. Several were occupied
and he had the feeling these were regular customers.

A long-haired gray cat was curled up atop a low coffee
table in one corner. Conan hurried immediately over to the
cat and Max braced himself for a confrontation but the two
of them seemed to have an understanding.

The cat sniffed, gave him a bored look, then sauntered
away just as a woman with a name badge that indicated she
worked at the store caught sight of them and hurried over
to greet Anna.

She looked thin and athletic, with long, salt-and-pepper
hair pulled back in a ponytail and round wire-rim glasses
that didn't conceal her glare.

"Excuse me, what are you doing here? Get out."

Anna tilted her head, much as the long-haired cat had
done. "Last I checked, I still own the place."

The older woman all but shook her finger at her. "This
is supposed to be your day off, missy. What do I have to
do, hide your van keys so you take some time off?"

Anna laughed and hugged the other woman. "Don't
nag. I know. I just brought the shipment of blown glass
floats that was delivered to the other store. They're all in
the back waiting to be stocked. You should see them,
they're every bit as gorgeous as the few samples we
received. I was afraid I wouldn't have time to drop them
off before court tomorrow and I know they're already a
week overdue."

"We would have gotten by without them for another
day or two."

"I know, but it was a lovely day for a drive. Sue Pop-
pleton, this is my new tenant, Lieutenant Harry Maxwell."

The woman gave him a friendly, curious smile, then turned back to Anna. "Since you're here, do you have five minutes to help me figure out what I'm doing wrong when I try to cancel a preorder in the system?"

"Of course. Max, do you mind just hanging out for a moment?"

"Not at all," he answered.

He headed for a nearby display of local travel books and was leafing through one on local history when he heard the front door chime. He didn't think much about it, until he realized the entire section of the store had gone deadly quiet.

Chapter Twelve

"Get out," he heard Anna say with a coldness in her voice Max had never heard before.

Conan growled suddenly—whether at her tone or at something else, Max had no idea but he now burned with curiosity.

Not knowing quite what to expect, he stepped away from the display so he could get a clear view of the door.

The man standing just inside the store didn't look threatening at all. He was one of those academic-looking types with smooth skin, artfully tumbled hair, intense eyes behind scholarly looking glasses. Exactly the sort one might expect to find sitting in a bookstore on a Sunday afternoon with a double espresso and the *New York Times* crossword puzzle.

So why the dramatic reaction? Conan was standing in front of Anna like he was all set to rip the man apart and even her employee looked ready to start chucking remaindered books at his head.

The guy seemed completely oblivious to their animosity, his gaze focused only on Anna.

"Come on, Anna. Cut me a break here. I was across the street at the coffee shop and saw your van pull up. I left an excellent croissant half-eaten in hopes you might finally give me a chance to explain."

"I don't need to hear any explanations from you. I need you out of my store right now."

Her voice wobbled, just a little, but in that instant Max figured it out. This must be the bastard who had screwed her over.

He took a step forward, thinking he could probably knock the guy out cold with one solid left hook, but he paused. Maybe it would be better to see how things played out.

Besides, she looked as if she had plenty of help.

"Call off your mutt, will you?"

The dog Max had never seen do anything but enthusiastically lick anyone who so much as looked at him still stood in a protective stance in front of Anna, low growls rumbling out of him.

"I ought to let him rip your throat out after what you've done."

"Come on, baby. Don't be like this."

He raked a hand through his hair and gave Anna what Max figured he probably thought was some kind of melting look.

Anna appeared very much frozen solid. "Like what?" she asked quietly. "Like a woman who finally found her brain about six months too late and figured out what a *cabrón* you are."

Max didn't know much Spanish but he'd heard that particular term in the army enough to know it was not a particularly affectionate or flattering one.

Sue chortled, which seemed to infuriate the man even

more. His face turned ruddy beneath his slick tan and he took a step forward, only to pause when Conan growled again.

His mouth hardened but he stopped. "How long did you have to practice that injured victim act you played so well in court when you testified?"

"Act?" Anna's voice rose in disbelief.

"Come on. You knew what was up the whole time. You just preferred to look the other way."

Anna drew in a shaky breath and even from here, Max could see the fury in her eyes. "Get out. That is your last warning before I call the police. I'm sure the judge will just love to find out you've been in here harassing me."

"Careful, babe. Harassment is an ugly word. You don't want to be throwing it around casually. Of course, sometimes it's a perfectly appropriate word. The exact one, really. Like when a business owner coerces an employee to sleep with her."

Her features paled and she looked vaguely queasy. "I never slept with you, thank the Lord."

"She didn't coerce you into anything and you know it, you disgusting piece of vermin," Sue snapped, and Fletcher blinked at her as if he'd forgotten she was there.

"Every single employee of By-the-Wind could testify about how you were the one constantly putting out the vibe, hitting on her every time she turned around," she went on. "Sending her flowers, writing poems on the employee bulletin board, taking credit for everybody else's ideas just so you could convince her you were Mr. Wonderful."

Anna drew in a deep breath, not looking at all thrilled by the other woman's defense of her. Instead, her color flared even higher. "Uh, Sue, maybe you should start unpacking those floats I brought so you can make sure none of them shattered in transit."

The other woman looked reluctant to leave but something

in Anna's gaze must have convinced her to go. With one last glare at Grayson Fletcher, she headed for the stockroom.

As soon as she was out of earshot, Anna turned back to the man. "You are way out of line."

He shrugged. "Maybe. But if, say, I spoke to the local newspaper reporter covering the case, I could probably spin things exactly my way. You wouldn't look like the sainted victim then, would you?"

Anna opened her mouth to retort, but he cut her off before she could. "Of course, I could always keep my mouth shut, under the right circumstances."

"What circumstances?"

He shrugged. "If I *am* convicted on these bogus charges, maybe, just maybe, you could see your way clear to testifying on my behalf in the sentencing hearing."

She narrowed her gaze. "That sounds suspiciously like blackmail."

"Another ugly word. That's not it at all. I would just think in the interest of making things right, you would want to tell the judge you've had second thoughts and have had time to look at things a little differently," he said calmly.

She gazed at him for a long time. Just before Max was ready to step forward and kick the guy out of the store, she spoke in a quiet, determined voice.

"Go to hell, Grayson. Of course, I can comfort myself with the thought that by this time next week that's exactly where you're going to find yourself—the hell that passes for the Oregon State Penitentiary in Salem."

The other man's face turned a mottled red, until any trace of anything that might have been handsome turned ugly and mean. He took another step forward, not even stopping when Conan barked sharply.

"You should have left things alone." His low, intense

voice dripped with rancor. "I would have paid everything back eventually. I was working on a plan. I tried to tell you that, but you were too damn uppity to listen. Well, you'll listen to me now. I have enough dirt on you that I can ruin you. You harassed me, you assaulted me, you threatened to fire me if I didn't sleep with you. That's the story I'm going to be feeding the pretty little local reporter. And then you framed me to hide your own crimes. When my civil suit is done, you're going to be lucky if I leave you with so much as a comic book. I'll take this store and your other one and that damn house you love so much. Then where will you be? A stone-cold bitch left with nothing."

She seemed to freeze, to shrink inside herself. Max, however, did not. He stepped away from the shelves and faced the other man down.

"Okay, time's up, bastard."

Anna lifted shocked eyes to his, as if she'd forgotten his presence. Max had dealt with enough of Fletcher's type in the military that he wasn't at all surprised to see his bullying bluster fade when confronted with direct challenge.

"Says who?" he asked warily.

"Between me and the dog, I think it's safe to say we can both make it clear you've outstayed your welcome."

Fletcher looked between Conan and Max, as if trying to figure out which of them posed the bigger threat, then he gave a hard laugh, regaining a little of his aplomb. "What are you going to do? Club me with your cast?"

Max gave the same grim, dangerous smile he used on recalcitrant trainees. "Try me."

The four of them stood in that tableau for several long seconds until Conan barked sharply, as if to add his two cents to the conversation. Fletcher stared at them again then gave Anna one last look of sheer loathing before he turned and stalked out of the store.

* * *

She wanted to die.

To walk down to the beach and dig the biggest, deepest hole she could manage and just bury herself inside it like a geoduck clam.

Bad enough that she had been caught unawares by Grayson and had stood there like an idiot letting him rant on and on with his damning—but completely ridiculous—allegations.

How much worse was it that Max had been a party to her disgrace?

Not exactly the best way to seduce a man, to show him unmistakable evidence what an idiot she was. When she remembered how she had actually thought she was coming to care for that piece of dirt, she just about thought she would be sick.

"Well, that was the single most humiliating ten minutes of my life."

Max moved closer and she alternated between wanting to bury her face in her hands so she didn't have to look at him and wanting to curl against that hard chest of his.

"You have no reason to feel humiliated. I'm the one who should feel humiliated. I didn't even get one good swing with my cast."

His disgruntled tone surprised a shaky laugh out of her. "I'm sure you can still chase him down at the bakery with his half-eaten croissant," she said. "Or send Conan over to bring him back."

"That kind of instant problem solving must be why you're the boss."

She laughed again, then realized her knees were wobbling. "Excuse me, I need to sit down."

She plopped down on the nearest couch, still fighting the greasy nausea in her belly, the sheer mortification that she had once been stupid and gullible enough to be attracted to a slimy worm like Grayson Fletcher.

"I told you my life was a mess."

"You've still got By-the-Wind."

"For now."

"Any chance he can make good on those threats?"

She sighed and pressed a hand to her stomach. Sexual harassment. How low could the man stoop?

"He can try, but there's absolutely no evidence backing him up. I refused to even date him for months. I didn't want any appearance of impropriety. The other employees can all confirm that. But he was so damn persistent and I was…flattered. That's what it comes down to. I only dated him for a month, but I swear I never slept with him."

Oh, why couldn't she keep her mouth shut? Did she really need to share that particular detail with Max?

"Then don't worry about it. I know his type. He's all bluff and bluster up front but the minute you confront him, he runs away like the rat he is."

"I'm just sorry you were tangled up in the middle."

"Funny, I was just thinking how glad I am that I was here to back you up."

She stared at him for a long moment, at the solid strength of his features, the integrity that seemed so much a part of him. The contrast between a sleazy, dishonest slimebag like Grayson Fletcher and this honorable soldier who had sacrificed so much for his country and still bore the scars for it was overwhelming.

"Thank you," she whispered.

With a full heart, she leaned across the space between them to kiss him softly. Compared to their heat and passion of the night before, this was just a tiny kiss of gratitude, just a slight brush of her lips against his, but it rocked her clear to her toes.

She was crazy about this man. She was aware she had only known him a few days but she was in serious danger of falling head over heels.

She eased away from him, feeling shaky and off balance.

"You're welcome," he murmured, and she wondered if she imagined that raspy note in his voice.

"What did I miss?"

At the sound of her employee's voice, Anna tried to collect her scattered wits. She took a deep breath and found Sue had come out of the stockroom carrying two of the colorful glass floats.

"Not much. He's gone."

"Good riddance. I don't care what you say, I'm calling the cops the next time he has the nerve to come in here."

"Sounds like a plan," Anna said. "Did I answer what you needed to know on canceling an order?"

"Yes. And now you need to get out of here and enjoy the rest of your day off." Sue had on that bossy mother-hen voice that Anna was helpless to fight. "Go have some fun. You deserve it."

She rubbed her hands on her slacks and turned back to Max as a customer came up to Sue and asked her for help locating an item.

"You're welcome to look around more if you'd like."

"I think I'm done here," he answered.

"Are you ready to go home, then?"

A strange light flickered in his eyes and she wondered at it, until she remembered his transitory life. The concept of home probably wasn't one he was used to considering.

"Good idea," he said after a moment, and his words were punctuated by Conan barking his approval.

* * *

Dusk was washing across the shore as they reached the outskirts of Cannon Beach and the setting sun cast long shadows across the road and saturated everything with color.

Brambleberry House on its hill looked graceful, welcoming, with its gables and gingerbread trim and the wide porch on all sides.

"I love coming home this time of day," she said as she pulled into the driveway. "I know it's silly but I always feel like the house has been waiting here all day just for me."

"It's not silly."

"Abigail used to say a house only comes alive when it's filled with people who love it." She smiled, remembering. "She used to have this quote on the wall. 'Every house where love abides and friendship is a guest, is surely home, and home, sweet home, for there the heart can rest.'"

He was quiet for a long time, gazing as she was at the house gleaming in the fading sunlight. "You do love it, don't you?" he asked, finally breaking the silence.

"With my whole heart. Rusty pipes, loose shingles, flaking paint and all."

"She knew what she was doing when she left it to you, didn't she?"

It seemed an odd question but she nodded. "I hope so. Sometimes I'm overwhelmed with the endless responsibility of it, especially when the rest of my life seems so chaotic right now. I have no idea why she left things as she did and bequeathed Brambleberry House to Sage and to me out of the blue, but I love it here. I can't imagine ever leaving."

He let out a breath, his eyes looking suddenly serious in the twilight. "Anna—"

Whatever he intended to say was lost when Conan began barking urgently from the cargo area of the van, as if he had expended every last ounce of patience.

She laughed. "Sorry. That sounds dire. I'd better take him down the beach a little to work out the kinks from the car ride. You interested?"

She thought she saw frustration flicker across his features but it was quickly gone.

"Sure. I've got kinks of my own to work out."

Conan leaped out of the van as soon as she hooked on his leash and practically dragged her behind him in his eagerness to mark every single clump of sea grass on the beach trail.

Just before they reached the wide stretch of beach, Max reached for her hand to help her around a rock and he didn't let go. They walked hand in hand with Conan ahead of them and warmth fluttered through her despite the cool spring wind.

She didn't want to the day to end. Even with the humiliation of the encounter with Gray Fletcher, it had been wonderful, the most enjoyable day she'd spent in longer than she could remember.

Conan obviously didn't share her sentiments, however. The dog could usually run for miles along the beach at any time of the day or night. But though he had been so insistent earlier, as soon as he had taken care of his pressing need, now he didn't seem nearly as enthusiastic to be walking. One moment he planted his haunches stubbornly in the sand, the next he tried to tug her back the direction they had come.

The third time he tried the trick, she gave a tug on the leash. "You don't know what you want, do you?"

"As a matter of fact, I do."

She looked over at Max and found him watching her in the fading sunlight, a glittery look in his hazel eyes that made her catch her breath.

"I was talking to Conan," she murmured. "He's being stubborn about the walk. I think he's ready to go back."

"Not yet," Max said quietly.

Before she could ask him why not, he pulled her against him as the sun slid farther down the horizon.

All the heat and wonder they had shared the night before during the storm came rushing back like the tide and she couldn't seem to get enough of him.

She tried to be careful of his sling and his arm but he lifted the sling out of the way so he could pull her against his chest.

He kissed her for long moments, until they were both breathing hard and the sun was only a pale rim on the horizon.

"If we keep this up, we're going to be stuck down here in the dark and won't be able to find our way back."

"Conan will lead the way," she murmured against his mouth. "He hasn't had dinner yet."

He laughed roughly and kissed her again. She wrapped her arms around his waist, a slow heat churning through her. She couldn't seem to get close enough to him, to absorb his hard strength and the safe harbor she felt here.

She didn't know how long they stood there accompanied by the murmur of the sea, a salty breeze eddying around them. She would have been quite content to stay all night if Conan hadn't finally barked with thinly veiled impatience.

The moon had started to rise above the coastal range, a thin sliver of light, but all was dark and mysterious around them.

"I guess we should probably head back."

She couldn't see his features but she was quite sure she sensed the same reluctance that was coursing through her.

Somehow she wasn't surprised when he pulled a flashlight from his keychain in the pocket of his leather bomber. He was a soldier, no doubt prepared for anything.

"I don't have night-vision goggles with me so this will have to do," Max said. He reached for her hand and they walked back up the beach toward Brambleberry House, whose lights gleamed a welcome in the darkness.

Her insides jumped wildly with nerves and anticipation. She didn't want this to end but how could she possibly scramble for the courage to tell him she wanted more?

They said little as they made their way back home. Even in his silence, though, she sensed he was withdrawing from her, trying to put distance between them again.

Her instinct was confirmed when they reached the house. She unlocked her apartment and opened the door for Conan to bound inside to find his food. She and Max stood in the foyer and she didn't miss the tight set of his features.

Desperate to regain the fleeting closeness, she drew in a shaky breath and lifted her mouth to his again.

After a moment's hesitation, he returned the kiss with an almost fierce hunger, until her thoughts whirled and her body strained against him.

After a long moment, he wrenched his mouth away. "Anna, I need to tell you something."

Whatever it was, she didn't want to hear it. Somehow she knew instinctively it was something she wouldn't like and right now she couldn't bear for anything to ruin the magic of this moment.

"Just kiss me, Max. Please."

He groaned softly but after a moment's hesitation he obliged, tangling his mouth with hers again and again until nothing else mattered but the two of them and the fragile emotions fluttering in her chest.

"I have been trying to figure out all day how to seduce you," she admitted softly.

His laugh was rough and strummed down her nerve endings. "I think it's safe to say you don't have to do anything but exist. That's more seduction than I can handle right now."

She smiled with the heady joy rushing through her. He made her feel delicate and beautiful, powerful in a way she had never known before.

"Come inside," she said, her voice soft.

He froze and she knew she didn't mistake the indecision on his features. "Anna, are you sure?"

"Please," she murmured.

With a ragged sigh, he yanked her against him and an exultant joy surged through her.

This was right. She was crazy about him, she thought. Head-over-heels crazy about this man.

She knew he wasn't going to be here forever, that he wanted to return to active duty as soon as possible and she would be alone again.

But for now, this moment, he was hers and she wasn't going to waste this precious chance fate had handed her.

A soft, silken spell wove around them as they kissed their way inside her bedroom.

The rest of her house was tasteful and subdued, all whites on wood tones. Her bedroom was different. It was soft and feminine, with lavenders and greens and yellows.

How was it possible that Max could seem so overwhelmingly masculine amid all the girly stuff, the flounces and frills? she wondered. He had never seemed so dangerously, enticingly male.

She led the way to her bed, with its filmy white hangings and mounds of pillows. Max looked at the bed for a moment then back at her and his expression was raw with desire.

"I should probably warn you I haven't done this in a while. I've been redshirted for a while with my injury and before that I was in a country where there wasn't a hell of a lot of opportunity for extracurricular activities."

She couldn't seem to think with these nerves skating through her. "Good to know. I haven't, either. My engagement ended five years ago and I haven't been with anyone else."

His eyes darkened, until the pupils nearly obscured the green-gray of the irises.

"I don't know if I can take things slowly. At least not the first time."

She smiled. "Good."

He gave a rough laugh and kissed her again, then lowered her to the bed. "As much as I want nothing more than to take hours undressing you and exploring every inch of that glorious skin, I'm a little clumsy with buttons right now. With this damn cast, I can barely work my own."

"I've got two hands," she answered. Her fingers trembled a little as she slowly worked the buttons of her shirt and pulled her arms free. At least she had worn one of her favorite bra-and-panty sets, a lacy creation in the palest peach.

He swallowed hard. "I definitely don't think I can take things slowly."

He pressed his mouth to her bared shoulder, then trailed kisses along the skin just above the scalloped edge of her bra. She shivered, arching against him as he slid a hand along the bared skin at her waist then up until he touched her intimately through the lace.

She wanted more. She wanted to feel his skin on hers. He must have shared her hunger because he pulled the sling off, revealing the cast underneath that ran from his wrist to just above his elbow and began working the buttons of his shirt.

"Let me help," she said.

He leaned back to give her more access and she helped him out of his shirt and then went to work on the snaps on his Levi's.

"I can take it from here," he told her.

In moments, they were both naked and he was everything she might have dreamed, all hard muscles and lean strength.

Then she caught her first view of the full extent of his injuries and her heart turned over in her chest.

For some reason, she had thought the damage was contained to his arm and shoulder. But rough, red-looking burns spread out from his collarbone to his pectoral muscles on the right side, crisscrossed by scars that were still blinding white against his skin.

"Oh, Max," she breathed.

Regret slid across his features. "I should have kept my shirt on. I'm so used to it by now I forget how ugly it is."

"No. No, you shouldn't have. I am so sorry you had to go through that."

She pressed her mouth just above the raw-looking skin at the spot where his shoulder met his neck, then again in the hollow above his collarbone.

"Does it hurt?"

He looked as if he wanted to deny it but he finally shrugged. "Sometimes. Right now, no. Right now, all I can think about is the incredibly sexy woman in my arms. Come up here and kiss me."

"Absolutely, Lieutenant," she said with a smile and settled in his arms.

They kissed and touched for a long time, exploring all the planes and hollows and secret places while those tensile emotions twisted through her, wrapping her closer to him.

He said he couldn't take things slowly but it seemed to her their teasing and touching lasted for hours. At last, when she wasn't sure she could endure another moment, he braced above her on his left forearm and he entered her.

She gasped his name and tightened her arms around him, hunger soaring inside her like bright, colorful kites on the wild air currents of the beach.

Had she ever known this sense of wonder, the feeling

of completion, that scattered pieces of herself had only right this moment fallen into place?

She was floating higher and higher, her heart as light as air as he moved inside her, slowly at first and then faster, his mouth hard and urgent on hers with a possessive stamp that thrilled her to the core.

She held tight to him, her body rising to meet his, and then he pushed slightly harder and she gasped suddenly as she broke free of gravity and went soaring into the air.

He groaned her name, then with one last powerful surge he joined her.

Oh, heaven. This was heaven. She held him tightly as a delicious lassitude slid over her.

Chapter Thirteen

Abigail would have approved.

Anna lay next to Max, her arm across him, feeling his chest rise and fall with each slow, steady breath as he slept. Pale moonlight filtered in through her open window and played across his features, and she thought how vulnerable he looked in sleep, years younger than the hard-eyed soldier he appeared at times.

Abigail would have loved him. She didn't quite know why she was so certain but somehow she knew her friend would have been quick to include him in the loose circle of friends that Sage had called her lost sheep—people who were lonely or tired or grieving or who just needed to know someone else believed in them.

Max would have been drawn into that circle, whether he wanted to or not. Abigail would have taken him in, would have filled him with good food to ease all the hollows from those months in the hospital. If he ended up leaving the army, Abigail would have been right there helping him figure out his place in the world.

He made a soft sound in his sleep and her arm tightened around him. She rested her cheek against his smooth, hard chest, astonished at the sense of peace she found here in his arms, the tenderness that seemed to wind through her with silken ties.

She was in love with him.

The truth shimmered through her, bright and stunning, and she drew in a sharp breath, astonished and suddenly terrified.

Love. That wasn't in the plan. She was supposed to be having a casual fling, nothing more. The man had made no secret of his plans to leave as soon as he could. This whole situation seemed destined for disaster.

He wasn't the stick-around type. He couldn't have made that more plain. He had told her himself that he considered his base in Iraq more of a home than anywhere else he had lived. She remembered how sad that had seemed when he told her. It was even more tragic now that she had come to know him better, since she had seen a certain yearning in his eyes when he looked at Brambleberry House.

He needs a home. A place to belong. That's what he's always needed.

The words whispered into her mind and she frowned. Why on earth would such a thought even enter her mind, let alone with such firm assurance? It made absolutely no sense, but she couldn't shake the unswerving conviction that Harry Maxwell needed Brambleberry House, maybe more even than she did.

She couldn't make him stay. She knew that with the same conviction. She might want him to, with sudden, fierce desperation, but she couldn't hold him here.

When his shoulder healed, he would return to his unit,

to his helicopter, and would go wherever he was needed, no matter how dangerous.

Even if his arm didn't heal as well as he hoped, she couldn't see him sticking around. Brambleberry House was a temporary stop on his life's journey and there was nothing she could do to change that.

She sighed, just a tiny breath of air, but it was enough to awaken him. Watching him come back to consciousness was a fascinating experience. No doubt it was the soldier in him but he didn't ease into wakefulness, he just instantly blinked his eyes open.

Her brothers always told her she did the same thing—one minute, she could be in deep REM sleep, the next she was wide-awake and ready to rock and roll.

They used to tease her that she slept with the proverbial one eye open, as if she was afraid one of them would sneak into her room during the night and steal her dolls. Not that she ever had many, but could she help it if she liked to protect what little she had from pesky older brothers?

"Hi," Max murmured, a sexy rasp to his voice, and Anna forgot all about brothers and dolls and sleeping.

"Hi yourself." She smiled, determined to savor every single moment she had with him. Why waste time wishing he could be a different sort of man, the kind who might be happy rattling around an old house like this for the rest of his life?

"Have I been asleep long?"

She shook her head. "A half hour, maybe."

"Sorry. I didn't mean to doze off on you."

"I didn't mind. It was…nice." A major understatement, but she wasn't about to risk scaring him off by revealing just how much she had treasured a quiet moment to savor being in his arms.

He gazed down at her, an oddly tender expression in his

hazel eyes that stole her breath and left her stomach doing cartwheels again.

"It has been. Everything. I never expected this, Anna. You have to know that."

She smiled, her heart full and light. "I didn't, either. But a gift can be all the more rare and precious when it's unexpected."

"Is that more of Abigail's wisdom?"

"No. Just mine."

With surprising dexterity, he tugged her with his left arm so she was lying across his chest, then he twisted his hand in her hair so he could angle her mouth to meet his kiss. "You are a wise woman, Anna Galvez."

She smiled. "I don't know about that. But I'm learning."

They kissed and touched and explored for a long time there in the dark, quiet intimacy of her room. At last he pulled her atop him, letting her set the pace.

Their first union had been all heat and fire. This was slower, sweet and sexy and tender all at the same time.

I love you.

She almost blurted the words just before she found release again, but she caught them in her throat before she could do something so foolish.

He wasn't ready to hear them yet—and she wasn't sure she was ready to say them.

It took a long time for his heartbeat to slow back to anything resembling a normal pace. He lay in the dark watching the moonlight dance across the room and listening to Anna breathe beside him.

The soft tenderness seeping through his insides scared the hell out of him.

This wasn't supposed to happen. He wasn't supposed to care so much. But somehow this woman, with her tough shell that he had discovered hid a fragile, vulnerable core, had become fiercely important to him.

She soothed him. He didn't know how she did it but these last few days with her had been filled with a quiet peace he only now realized had been missing since his helicopter crashed.

He had been so damn restless since he was injured. But with Anna, the future didn't seem like a scary place anymore. She made him think he could handle whatever came along.

Except telling her the truth.

He let out a long, slow breath, guilt pinching away at the tranquility of the moment. He had to tell her Abigail was his aunt. The very fact that he was lying in her bed having this conversation with himself while she was naked and warm in his arms was evidence that he had allowed the deception to go on far too long.

But how, exactly, was he supposed to tell her that now? She would be furious and hurt, especially after they had shared this.

He stared up at the ceiling, trying to figure out his options. He ached at the idea of hurting her but he couldn't see any way out of it. Maybe it would be best all the way around if he just left town before this could go on any further.

She would be hurt and baffled if he suddenly disappeared. But what would hurt her more—wondering why he left or discovering he had deceived her, that he had slept with her under false pretenses?

What he had done was unconscionable. He could fool himself that his intentions had been honorable, that he had only wanted to make sure Abigail had been competent in her last wishes when she left the house to Anna and Sage Benedetto. He had been compelled to do something, if only to assuage his own guilt over his negligence these last few years.

Then he had come to Brambleberry House and Anna had made Abigail's French toast for him and bandaged his wounds and kissed him senseless and everything had become so damn tangled.

He hated the idea of leaving her. It seemed the height of cowardice, especially after what they had shared tonight. But what would cause the least harm to her?

"Will you come with me next week when the verdict is read?"

Her voice in the darkness startled him and he shifted his gaze from the ceiling to see her watching him out of those huge dark eyes.

"I thought you were asleep," he said.

"No. I was just thinking."

"About the trial?"

"Sorry. Everything comes back to that right now. I'll be so glad when it's over."

He kissed her forehead, pulling her into a more comfortable position. "It's been rougher on you than you let on, hasn't it?"

She didn't answer but he thought her arms tightened around him. "I've been okay. I have. I just…I think I could use someone else in my corner during the verdict. Would you come?"

Like his aunt, Anna was a strong, independent woman. He had a feeling asking for anything was difficult for her. The fact she had asked him to stand by her touched him deeply.

He could stay a few more days. He owed her that, and perhaps giving her the support she needed at this critical time would be a small way to atone for his deception.

"Yeah. Sure. I'll come with you," he answered. "And if he's found not guilty, we've always got clubbing him senseless with my cast to fall back on as Plan B."

She laughed and kissed him. He pulled her close, pushing away the chiding voice of his conscience for now.

A few more days of this sweet, seductive peace. That's all he wanted. Surely that wasn't too much to ask.

"Are you ready for this?" Max asked her three days later as they sat on a park bench outside her store in Lincoln City enjoying the afternoon sunshine, the first since Sunday.

She made a face, her stomach fluttering with nerves. "Do I have a choice?"

"You always have a choice. You could just forget the whole thing and catch the next fishing boat out of town. Or I could make a phone call, get us a helicopter in here to fly us down the coast to an excellent crab shack I've heard about in Bandon."

"You're not helping."

He gave her an unrepentant grin and she couldn't help thinking how much lighter he had seemed these last few days. The occasional shadow still showed up in his gaze but he laughed more and seemed far more comfortable with the world.

The time they'd spent together since Sunday night had seemed magical. She never would have expected it, but the last two days of the trial passed with amazing swiftness. Even listening to the defense's closing arguments, where she had been painted as everything from an incompetent manager to a corrupt manipulator, hadn't stung as much as it might have a few days earlier.

Now she saw it for what it was—Grayson's desperate ploy to escape justice.

Between the trial and trying to stay on top of administrative duties at both stores, her days had been as packed and chaotic as always.

But the nights.

They had been sheer heaven.

When she returned to Brambleberry House Monday night, Max and Conan had been waiting for her with what he called his specialty—take-out Chinese. After dinner, Max started a fire in her fireplace and read a thriller with Conan at his feet while Anna did payroll and caught up on paperwork.

Eventually she gave up trying to concentrate with all this heat jumping through her insides. She had joined him on the couch and Max had tossed her reading glasses aside and kissed her while rain clicked against the window and Conan snored softly beside them. Later—much later—she had fallen asleep holding his hand.

Tuesday had been largely a repeat, except he had grilled steaks for her out in the rain while she held an umbrella over his head and laughed at the picture he made in one of Abigail's frilly flowered aprons.

That was the moment she knew with certainty that what she felt for him wasn't some passing infatuation, that she was hopelessly in love with him—with this wounded soldier with the slow smile and the secrets in his eyes.

She had no idea what she was going to do about it—except for now, she was going to live in the moment and enjoy every second she had with him.

Her cell phone rang suddenly and she jumped and stared at it.

"Are you going to get that?" Max asked.

"I'm working up to it."

She knew it must be the prosecutor, calling to tell her the verdict was in and about to be read.

The jury had been deliberating for four hours and Max had been with her for two of those hours. She had called him as soon as the jury had started deliberations and he had rushed down to Lincoln City immediately, even after she told him it might be hours—or possibly days—before the jurors reached a verdict.

She was immeasurably touched that he had kept his promise to come with her when the verdict was read—and she was grateful now as she answered her phone with fingers that trembled.

"Hello?" she said.

"They're back," the prosecutor said. "Can you be here in fifteen minutes?"

"Yes. I'll be right there."

She hung up the phone and sat, feeling numb and shaky at the same time.

Max reached for her hand. "Come on. I'll drive your car. We can come back for mine."

He kept his hand linked with hers as they walked into the courthouse. "What will you do if he's exonerated?" he asked, the question she had been dreading.

A few days ago, she was quite certain that possibility would have devastated her. But she had learned she had a great deal in common with Abigail's favorite sea creatures. Like the by-the-wind sailors her store was named for, she would float where fate took her and manage to adapt. Even on that fishing boat Max joked about.

"I'll survive," she said. "What else can I do?"

He squeezed her fingers and didn't let go as they walked into the courtroom and sat down.

So much of her life the last several months had been tied up with this trial but in the end, the verdict was almost anti-climactic. When the jury foreman read that jurors had found Grayson Fletcher guilty on all counts of fraud, Anna let out a tiny sob of relief and Max immediately wrapped her in his arms and kissed her.

Max stayed by her side as she hugged the prosecutor, who had worked so tirelessly for conviction, and as she received encouraging words from several others in the community who had come to hear the verdict.

She finally allowed herself to glance at Grayson and found him looking pale and stunned, as if he couldn't quite believe it was real. A tiny measure of pity flickered through her, even though she knew he deserved the consequences for what he had done.

Still, she wasn't going to hold a grudge the rest of her life, she decided. Life was just too short for her to be bitter and angry at being duped.

"We need to celebrate," Max said after they left the courtroom. "I'm taking you to dinner tonight. Where would you like to go?"

"The Sea Urchin," she said promptly, without taking even a moment to think about her answer. "Sage's husband owns it and since it's a Spencer Hotels property, of course it's fabulous. The food there is unbelievable. The best on the coast."

"I love a woman who knows what she wants."

If only he truly meant his words, she thought, then pushed the thought away. She was deliriously happy right now and she wasn't going to spoil it by worrying about the future.

She had a hard-and-fast rule never to use her cell phone while she was driving except in an absolute emergency, especially on the sometimes curvy coastal road, but she was severely tempted as she drove her van home from Lincoln City to phone everyone in her address book to give them the happy news.

She restrained herself, focusing instead on following Max's SUV, since they had both driven down separately, and trying to contain the happiness bubbling through her.

Still, even before she had a chance to greet Conan, her cell phone rang the moment she walked in the door at

Brambleberry House. She grinned when she saw Sage's name and number on the caller ID.

"All right, that's just spooky. How did you know the verdict was in?" she asked, without even saying hello.

Sage shrieked. "It is? I had no idea! Sue called me from the store hours ago when the jury went out for deliberation. I was just checking the status of things since I haven't heard from you. Tell me!"

Anna took a deep breath, thinking again how her life had changed since she inherited this house. A year ago, she would have had no one to share this excitement with except her employees. Now she had dear friends who loved her. She was truly a lucky woman.

"Guilty. Guilty, guilty, guilty!"

"Yes!" She heard Sage shouting the news to Eben and even over the phone, Anna could hear her husband's delighted exclamation.

"Oh, that's wonderful news. I hope they throw the book at the little pissant."

"This, from the world's biggest bleeding heart?" she teased.

"I care about things that deserve my time and energy," Sage said primly. "Grayson Fletcher does not."

"True enough," Anna replied.

"Oh, I'm so happy. I'm only sorry I wasn't there. With Julia gone, too, you're not going to have anyone to celebrate with!"

"Am, too," she answered. "For your information, I'm going to the Sea Urchin for dinner with Max."

There was a long, pregnant silence on the other end of the phone. "Max? Upstairs Max?"

Anna smiled, wondering how he would react to that particular nickname. "That's right."

"All right. What other secrets have you been keeping from me, you sly thing?"

Anna grimaced. She probably shouldn't have let that slip. But now that she had, she knew she wouldn't be able to fool Sage for long. "Nothing. Well, not much, anyway. It's just that Upstairs Max has been spending most of his time downstairs the last few days," she finally confessed.

That long pause greeted her again. "So does Conan like him?"

"Adores him. He treats him like his long-lost best friend."

"And have you smelled any freesia lately?"

Anna made a face. "Cut it out. Abigail's not matchmaking in this situation. She must be taking a break."

"Or maybe he's not the one for you."

Her heart gave a sharp little tug. "Of course he's not," she answered promptly. "He's only here a short time and then he's leaving again. I know that perfectly well."

"Are you sure?"

She wasn't certain of anything, other than that she was fiercely in love with Harry Maxwell. But she wasn't about to reveal that little tidbit of information to Sage.

"You know I'm going to insist on a full report from Julia as soon as she gets back. And the minute we get back to the States, I'm coming up there, even if I have to use up all my carbon offsets for the year."

"Sage, honey, stop worrying about me, okay? You don't have to come up here to babysit me. Max is a wonderful man and I know you'll love him. But I also know this is only temporary. I'm fine with that."

After she hung up the phone some time later, those words continued to echo through her mind. Had she ever lied to Sage before? She couldn't remember. This one was a doozy, though. She wasn't fine. No matter how cool and sophisticated she tried to be about things, she knew she would be devastated when he left.

And he would leave. She knew that, somewhere deep

inside of her, with a certainty she couldn't explain. Her time with him was limited. Even now, he could be preparing to leave.

Fight for him. He needs you.

The words whispered through her mind, so strong and compelling that she looked around the room to find a source.

He needs you.

The smell of freesia floated across the room and Conan looked up from his rug, thumped his tail on the floor, then went back to sleep.

Anna shivered, her heart pounding, then she quickly caught herself before her imagination went crazy. That's what happened when she talked to Sage. She lost every ounce of common sense and started believing in ghosts.

Not that it was bad advice. If she loved Max, shouldn't she be willing to fight for the man?

Starting tonight, she decided, and went to her closet for her favorite dress, a shimmery sheath in pale green that made her dark skin and hair look exotic and sultry.

She might not have a matchmaking ghost on her side, but she could take control of her own fate.

Max wouldn't know what hit him.

Chapter Fourteen

Max rang the doorbell to Anna's apartment, aware of the sense of foreboding in his gut.

He was going to tell her tonight after dinner. No more excuses. He had put things off far too long and the time had come to confess everything. Maybe she would be so happy at the guilty verdict that she would be in a forgiving sort of mood.

Or maybe she would evict him and throw all his belongings out of her house.

He hoped not. He hoped she would find it in her to understand his motives. But either way, he owed her the truth.

Conan barked behind the door and a moment later, it swung open, revealing a vision in pale green.

From the first time he saw her, Max had considered Anna Galvez beautiful, with those huge brown eyes and her glossy dark hair and classically lovely features.

But right now she was truly breathtaking.

She had piled her hair up in a loose, feminine style, with curls dripping everywhere. She wore a sexy dream of a dress with a low back that showed off fine-boned shoulders and all that luscious skin of hers. She also wore more jewelry than he'd seen on her—a diamond choker and matching bracelet and slim, dangly earrings that glittered in the foyer light.

She looked lush and sensual and he wanted to stand in the foyer of Brambleberry House all night just looking at her.

"Wow," he murmured. "You look incredible. I know that sounds completely lame but I can't think of another word for it."

"Incredible is good." She smiled. "Come in. I'm just about ready."

He wanted to devour her but he was afraid of messing up perfection so he stood inside the doorway while she picked up a filmy scarf from a side table and wrapped it around her shoulders, then grabbed one of those tiny little evening bags women managed to cram huge amounts of paraphernalia into.

Conan padded over to her wearing one of his pathetic take-me-with-you looks. The dog brushed against her and Max held his breath. Meredith—hell, most women he knew—would have gone ballistic to have dog hairs on one of her fancy party dresses but Anna simply laughed and scratched the dog's chin.

"I'm sorry, bud, but you know you can't go with us to the Sea Urchin. You wouldn't want to. You'd be bored senseless, I promise. But we'll be back later and we'll play then."

The dog heaved a massive sigh and headed for his favorite rug, but in that instant, that tiny interaction, Max felt as if the entire house had just collapsed on top of him.

Emotions washed through him, thick and raw and terrifying, and for an instant of panic, he wanted to turn on his heels and walk out of Brambleberry House and just keep on going.

He was in love with Anna Galvez. Not because she was achingly beautiful or because she made his heart race and the blood pool in his gut.

But because she was strong and courageous and smart and she made him believe in himself again.

He was in love with her. How the hell had that happened?

One minute, his life had been going along just fine. Okay, maybe not perfect. His shoulder problems were proving to be a major pain and he had no idea if he would still be in the army in a few weeks. But he had been dealing with the setbacks in his own way.

And then this woman, with her stubborn independence and her brilliant smile and her ambitious dreams, had knocked him on his butt. She talked to her dog and she knew her way around a wood chipper and she filled his soul with a peace he never realized had been missing.

"Max? Is everything okay?"

How long had he been staring at her? Too long, obviously. He drew in a ragged breath and realized she was watching him with concern while Conan seemed to be grinning at him.

"Yeah. Yeah. Fine. You just dazzle me."

He could tell she thought he was talking about her appearance and he decided not to correct the misconception.

"Thank you." She smiled. "The jewelry is Abigail's. She never went anywhere, even to the grocery store, without glittery stuff dripping from every available surface. She used to tell me, 'My dear girl, a woman my age has to use every available means at her disposal to distract the eye from all these wrinkles.'"

He could hear Abigail saying exactly that and he suddenly missed his aunt desperately.

"You don't need any jewels," he said. "You're stunning enough without them. The most beautiful woman I've ever known."

Her mouth parted slightly as her eyes softened. "Oh, Max," she whispered. "I do believe that's the sweetest thing anyone has ever said to me."

"It's the truth," he said gruffly.

She smiled with stunning sweetness and stepped forward to press her mouth against his.

His heart seemed to flop around in his chest like a rockfish on the line and he could barely breathe around the tenderness inside him. He kissed her, almost desperate with the need to touch her, taste her, burn every moment of this in his mind.

The magic he always found with her began to coil and twine around them and he closed his eyes as she wrapped her arms around his neck, holding him as if she couldn't bear to let go.

He was wondering just how long it might take for her to fix herself up again if he messed up all this perfection when Conan suddenly barked urgently and raced to the door.

A moment later, he heard the front door to the house open and children's laughter echo through the house.

Anna pulled away from him with a startled gasp, then her face lit up with joy. If she was breathtaking before, right now with her eyes bright and a wide smile lighting her features, she was simply staggering.

"They're back!" she exclaimed.

He couldn't seem to make his brain work. "Who?"

"Julia and the twins! Oh, this just makes this entire day perfect. Come on, you've got to meet them."

She looked a little windblown from the passion of their kiss but she linked her hand with his and opened the door. Conan rushed out first, just about tripping over his feet in his rush to greet two dark-haired children who were starting up the stairs, their arms loaded with backpacks.

"Conan!" both children shouted, dropping their bundles and hurrying back down the stairs.

The dog barked and jumped around them, licking first one and then the other while the boy and girl giggled and hugged him.

"Hey, I need a little of that love."

"Anna Banana!"

The little boy jumped up from hugging the dog and launched himself at Anna. She gave him a tight hug then turned to gather the less rambunctious girl to her as well.

"How are you, my darlings? I know you've only been gone a week, but I swear you've grown a foot in that time! What have you been eating, Maddie? Ice cream for breakfast, lunch and dinner?"

The girl giggled and shook her head. "Nope. Only for breakfast and lunch. We had pizza and cheeseburgers the rest of the time."

"You've been living large in Montana, haven't you?"

"We had tons of fun, Anna! You should have come with us! We went on a horseback ride and we went sledding and skiing and then we went to Boise and visited Grandma and Grandpa for three whole days," the boy exclaimed.

The girl—Maddie—dimpled at her. "You look super-pretty, Anna. Are you going to a ball?"

Anna smiled and hugged her again. "No, sweetheart. Just to dinner at Chloe's dad's hotel."

"Ooh, will you bring me a fortune cookie?" the boy asked. "I love their fortune cookies."

"I'll see what I can do," Anna promised, just as a slim blond woman tromped through the door carrying a suitcase in each arm. She dropped them as soon as she walked into the foyer and saw Anna greeting the children, and Max watched while the two women embraced.

"I just heard. Sage just called me. Oh, Anna, I'm so happy about the guilty verdict. Will is, too."

"Yeah," Maddie said with a grin. "You should have heard him yelling in the car. My ears still hurt!"

Anna laughed and looked behind them. "Where is Will?"

"He's getting the rest of our luggage off the roof rack. He should be here in a moment."

The woman glanced over Anna's shoulder at Max and though she gave him a friendly smile, he thought he saw a kind of protective wariness there. It made him wonder what Anna might have told her friends about him.

"Hi," she said. "You must be Harry Maxwell."

The false name scraped against his conscience like metal on metal. He didn't know what to say, loathe to perpetuate the lie any more than he already had.

Anna saved him from having to come up with a response. "I'm sorry," she exclaimed with a distracted laugh. "I was so happy to see you all again, I forgot my manners. Max, this is Julia Blair and her children Maddie and Simon. Julia, this is Lieutenant Harry Maxwell."

He nodded hello, then reached forward to shake Julia's outstretched hand.

"We're interrupting something, aren't we?" she said. "You both look wonderful and you're obviously on your way out."

"We're heading to the Sea Urchin to celebrate the verdict," Anna said.

"We can do it another time," Max offered. "I'm sure you two probably want to catch up."

"No, go on. Keep your plans," Julia said. "We can catch up later tonight over tea when the kids are in bed."

Max said nothing, though he thought with fleeting regret of the last two nights when he had slept with her in his arms.

"I was going to shut Conan in my apartment while we're at dinner but you're certainly welcome to take him upstairs with you. I'm sure he'll be so much help while you're trying to unpack."

"Thanks," the other woman said dryly.

"Let me help you with your luggage," Max said.

Julia gave a surprised glance at his omnipresent sling. "You don't have to do that."

"You'd better let him," Anna said with a laugh. "The man doesn't take no for an answer."

"Doesn't he?" Julia murmured.

Max felt his face heat and decided he would be wise to beat a hasty retreat. He picked up one of the suitcases and carried it up and set it on the landing outside the second-floor apartment. He was just heading back down for the second suitcase, when he heard a male voice from the foyer below.

"We were only gone eight days. Why, again, did we need all these suitcases?"

Max froze on the stairway, his heart stuttering. He knew the owner of that voice.

And worse, the man knew him.

"Wow, Anna. You look fabulous!"

Anna beamed at Will Garrett, who lived three houses down. Will was not only a gifted carpenter who had done most of the renovation work on Brambleberry House but, more importantly, he was a dear friend.

"I would say the same for you if I could see you behind all the suitcases," she said with a laugh.

"Here. How's that?" He set down the luggage and pulled her into a close hug. She hugged him back, her heart lifting at the smile he gave her. Every time she saw Will, she marveled at the changes in him these last six months since he and Julia had fallen in love again.

Before Julia and her twins came to Brambleberry House, Will had been a far different man. He had been lost in grief for his wife and daughter who had been killed in a car accident three years ago.

Anna had grieved with him for Robin and Cara. She and Sage—and Abigail, before her death—had worried for him as he pulled away from their close circle of friends, drawing inside himself in the midst of his terrible pain.

They had all rejoiced when Julia moved in upstairs and they learned she had been his first love, when they were just teenagers.

The two of them had rediscovered that love and together, Julia and her twins had helped Will begin to heal.

"I heard the good news about that idiot Fletcher," Will said, too low for the children to overhear. "I couldn't be happier that he's finally getting what's coming to him. Maybe now you can put the whole thing behind you and move forward."

She thought of the progress she had made, how she had brooded far too long about everything. Her perspective had changed these last few days, she realized, thanks in large part to Max.

She *was* ready to move forward, to refocus her efforts on saving both stores. Through hard work, she had built something good and worthwhile. She couldn't just give up all that because of a setback like Gray Fletcher.

She looked up and saw Max standing motionless on the stairs. She smiled up at him, awash in gratitude for these last few days and the confidence he had helped her find again.

"I need to introduce you to our new tenant. Will, this is—"

He followed her gaze and suddenly his eyes lit up. "Max! What are you doing here?"

Max walked slowly down the stairs and Anna frowned when Will gave him that shoulder tap thing men did that seemed the equivalent to the hug of greeting she and Julia had shared.

"Why didn't anybody tell me you were living upstairs? This is wonderful news. Abigail would have been thrilled that you've finally come home."

Anna stared between the two men. Will looked delighted, while Max's expression had reverted to that stony, stoic look he had worn so often when he first arrived at the house.

Her pulse seemed unnaturally loud in her ears as she tried to make sense of this new turn of events. "I don't understand," she finally said. "You two know each other?"

"Know each other? Of course!" Will exclaimed. "We hung out all the time, whenever he would visit his aunt. A couple weeks every summer."

"His…aunt?"

Will gave her an odd look. "Abigail! This is her nephew. The long-lost soldier, Max Harrison."

Anna drew in a sharp breath, her solar plexus contracting as if someone had socked her in the gut. She stared at Max, who swallowed hard but didn't say anything.

"That's impossible," she exclaimed. "Abigail's nephew's name was Jamie. Not Harry or Max. *Her Jamie.* That's what she always called him."

"My full name is Maxwell James Harrison. Abigail was the only one who called me Jamie."

She was going to hyperventilate for the first time in her life. She could feel the breath being slowly squeezed from her lungs. "Max Harrison—Harry Maxwell. I'm such an idiot. Why didn't I figure it out?"

"I can explain if you'll let me."

Lies. Everything they shared was lies. She had kissed him, held him, slept with him, for heaven's sake. And it had all been a lie.

She pressed a hand to her stomach, to the nausea curling

there. First Grayson and now Max. Did she wear some invisible sign on her forehead that said Gullible Fool Here?

All her joy in the day, the triumph of the guilty verdict, the fledgling hope that she could now regain her life seemed to crumble away like leaves underfoot.

Julia, with her usual perception, must have sensed some of what was racing through Anna's head. She quickly stepped in to take control of the situation.

"Will, kids, let's get these suitcases out of the entryway and upstairs to the apartment. Come on."

The children grumbled but they grabbed their backpacks and trudged up the stairs, Conan racing ahead of them in his excitement at having them all back.

In moments, the chaos and bustle of their homecoming was reduced to a tense and ugly silence as she gazed at the man she thought she had fallen in love with.

Most people call me Max. She remembered his words, which very well might have been the only honest thing he had said to her since he moved in.

She moved numbly back into her apartment, only vaguely aware that he had followed her inside.

A hundred thoughts raced through her head but she could only focus on one.

"You lied to me."

"Yes," he answered. Just that, nothing else.

"What am I missing here?" she asked. "Why would you possibly feel like you had to lie about your relationship with Abigail and use a false name?"

He rubbed a hand at the base of his neck. "It was a stupid idea. Monumentally stupid. All I can say is that it seemed like a good idea at the time."

"That tells me nothing! Who wakes up in the morning and says, 'gosh, I think I'll create a false identity today, just for kicks'?"

"It wasn't like that."

"Then explain it to me!"

Her hands were shaking, she realized. This felt worse than the slick, greasy feeling in her stomach when her accountant had discovered the first hint of wrongdoing at the store. She was very much afraid she was going to be sick and she did her best to fight down the nausea.

"I was stationed in Fallujah when Abigail died. I didn't even know she died until several months later."

"Wrong!" she exclaimed. "Sage notified Abigail's family. I know she did! Not that it did any good. Not a single family member bothered to come to her funeral."

"Sage notified my mother. Not the same thing at all. I told you my relationship with my mother is difficult at best and she never liked Abigail. The only reason she let me come here all those summers was because she thought Abigail was loaded and would eventually leave everything to me. Meredith didn't think to mention to me that Abigail had even died until two months after the fact, and then only in passing."

"How can I believe anything you tell me?"

He closed his eyes. "It's true. I loved Abigail. I doubt I could have swung leave to attend a great-aunt's funeral but I would have moved heaven and earth to try."

"So how do we get from here to there?"

He sighed. "My mother is between husbands, which means that, as usual, she's short on cash. She suddenly remembered Abigail had this house that was supposed to be worth a fortune and she seemed to think it should have come to me, as Abigail's only living relative. And of course, to her by default if something happened to me in the Middle East. Imagine her dismay when she found out Abigail had left Brambleberry House to someone else. Two strangers."

The nausea roiled in her stomach, mostly that he could speak of his own mother regarding his possible demise with such callousness. "This was about money?"

"I don't give a damn about the money!" he said, with unmistakable vehemence. "My mother might but I don't. This was about making sure Abigail knew what she was doing when she left the house and its contents to two complete strangers."

"Strangers to you, maybe, but not to Abigail!" Anna's temper flared with fierce suddenness. "She was our friend. Sage and I both loved her dearly and she loved us. Obviously more than she loved some nephew who never even bothered to visit her."

He drew in a sharp breath. "It was a little tough to find time for social calls when I was in the middle of a damn war zone!"

She had hurt him, she realized. She wanted to take back her words but how could she, when her insides were being ripped apart by pain?

She loved him and he had lied to her, just like every other man she'd ever been stupid enough to trust.

She could feel hot tears burning behind her eyes and she was very much afraid she was going to break down in front of him, something she absolutely could not allow. She blinked them back, focusing on the anger.

"Let me get this straight. You came here because you thought I was some kind of scam artist? That Sage and I had schemed and manipulated our way into Abigail's life so she would leave us the legacy that should have been yours."

He compressed his mouth into a tight line. "Something like that."

"And where did sleeping with me fit into that?"

Chapter Fifteen

Her words hovered between them, a harsh condemnation of his actions these last few days. In her eyes, he could see her withdrawal, the hurt and fury he fully deserved.

Why had he ever been stupid enough to think coming to Cannon Beach was a good idea? He thought of the events he had set into motion by that one crazy decision. He hated most of all knowing he had hurt her.

"Everything between us has been a lie," she said, her voice harsh.

"Not true." He stepped forward, knowing only that he needed some contact with her, but she took a swift step back and he fought hard to conceal the pain knifing through him.

"I never expected any of this to happen. I only intended to spend a few weeks running recon here, getting the lay of the land. I just wanted to check things out, make sure everything was aboveboard. I felt like I owed it to Abigail because…"

Because I loved her and I never had a chance to say goodbye.

"Well, my reasons don't really matter. I swear, I tried to keep my distance but you made it impossible."

"What did I do?"

"You invited me to breakfast," he said simply.

You fixed up my scrapes and bruises, you listened with compassion when I rambled on about my scars, you kissed me and lifted me out of myself.

You made me fall in love with you.

The words clogged in his throat. He wanted desperately to say them but he knew she wouldn't welcome them. He had lost any right to offer her his love.

"I figured out a long time ago that you genuinely cared about Abigail and there was nothing underhanded in you and Sage Benedetto inheriting Brambleberry House."

"Well, that's certainly reassuring to know. Was that before or after you slept with me?"

"Anna—"

"So tell me, Max. As soon as you figured out I wasn't some con artist, why didn't you tell me who you were?"

He raked a hand through his hair. "I wanted to, a hundred times. I tried, but something always stopped me. The dog. The storm. I don't know. It just never seemed like the right time."

He sighed, wishing she would give him even the tiniest of signals that she believed any of this. "And then after we made love, I felt like we were so entangled, I didn't know how to tell you without hurting you."

Her laugh was bitter and scorched his heart. "Far easier to go on letting stupid, oblivious Anna believe the fantasy."

"You're not stupid. Or oblivious. I deceived you. Though I might have thought I had good intentions, that I owed something to Abigail's memory, it was completely wrong of me to let things go as far as they did."

She said nothing and he scanned her features, looking for any softening but he saw nothing there but pain and anger. "I never meant to hurt you," he said.

She stood in a protective stance with her shoulders stiff, and her arms wrapped tightly around her stomach, and he didn't know how to reach her.

"Isn't it funny how people always say that after the fact?" she said, her voice a low condemnation. "If you truly never meant to hurt me, you should have told me you were Abigail's nephew after you kissed me for the first time."

He had no defense against the bitter truth of her words. She was absolutely right.

He had no defense at all. He was wrong and he had known it all along.

"I'm sorry," he murmured, hating the inadequacy of the words but unable to come up with anything better. He should leave, he thought. Just go before he made things worse for her.

He headed to the door but before he opened it, he turned back and was struck again by how beautiful she was. Beautiful and strong and forever out of his reach now.

"Aunt Abigail knew exactly what she was doing when she left Brambleberry House to you," he said, his voice low. "She would have hated to see me sell this house she loved so much and she must have known that with my career in the army, I wouldn't have been able to give it the love and care you have. You belong here, in a way I never could."

He closed the door softly behind him and headed slowly up the stairs, every bone in his body suddenly aching to match the pain in his heart.

That last he had said to her was a blatant lie, just one more to add to the hundreds he had told.

She belonged here, that much was truth. But he couldn't tell her that these last few days, he had begun to think perhaps he could also find a place here in this house that had always been his childhood refuge.

The words to the poem she had quoted echoed through his memory. *Every house where love abides and friendship is a guest, is surely home, and home, sweet home, for there the heart can rest.*

His heart had come to rest here, with Anna. She had soothed his restless soul in ways he still didn't quite understand. He had come here hurting and guilty over the helicopter crash and the deaths of his team members, wondering what he could have done differently to prevent the crash.

He had been frustrated about his shoulder, worried about the future, grieving for his team and for Abigail.

But when he was with Anna, he found peace and comfort. She had helped him find faith again, faith in himself and faith in the future.

The thought of walking away from her, from this place, filled him with a deep, aching sorrow. But what choice did he have?

He couldn't stay here. He had made that impossible. He had been stupid and selfish and he had ruined everything.

"How is it humanly possible for one woman to be such a colossal idiot when it comes to men?"

Two hours after Max walked out of her apartment, Anna sat in Julia's kitchen. The children were in bed, exhausted from their journey, and Will had returned to his own home down the beach, the house where he and Julia would live after their marriage in June.

"That is a question we may never answer in our lifetimes." Sage's voice sounded tinny and hollow over the speakerphone.

"Sage!" Julia exclaimed, a frown on her lovely features.

"Kidding. I'm kidding, sweetheart. You know I'm kidding, Anna. You're not an idiot. You're the smartest woman I've ever met."

"So why do I keep falling for complete jerks?"

Conan whined from his spot on the kitchen rug and gave her a reproving look similar to the one Julia had given the absent Sage.

"Are you sure he's a complete jerk?" Julia's voice was quiet. "He is Abigail's nephew, after all, so he can't be all bad. I've been wracking my memory and I think I might have met him a time or two when we stayed here during the summers when I was a girl. He always seemed very polite. Quiet, even."

"I'm afraid I never met him so I can't really offer an opinion either way," Sage said on the phone. "He came to stay several years ago before he shipped out to the gulf but I was on a field survey down the coast the whole time. I do know Abigail always spoke about him in glowing terms, but I figured she was a little biased."

Anna remembered the solid assurance she had experienced several times that Abigail would have approved of Max and her growing relationship with him. It hadn't been anything she could put her finger on, just a feeling in her heart.

Fight for him. He needs you.

She suddenly remembered those thoughts drifting through her mind earlier in the evening when she had been preparing for the celebration that hadn't happened.

She was almost certain that had been a figment of her imagination. But was it possible Abigail had been trying to give her some kind of message?

She hated this. She couldn't trust him and she certainly couldn't seem to trust herself.

"He lied to me, just like Gray and just like my fiancé.

With my history, how can I get past that?" she asked out loud as she set her spoon back in the bowl of uneaten ice cream.

She hadn't had much of an appetite for it in the first place but now the cherry chocolate chunk tasted terrible with this bitterness in her mouth.

"Maybe you can't," Sage said.

Julia said nothing, though an expression of doubt flickered over her features.

"You don't agree?" Anna asked.

The schoolteacher shrugged. "Do I think he should have told you he was Abigail's nephew? Of course. Deceiving you was wrong. But maybe he just found himself in a deep hole and he didn't know how to climb out without digging in deeper."

"And maybe he should have just buried himself in the hole when he got down far enough," Sage said.

Though Anna knew Sage was only trying to offer her support, she suddenly found she wanted to defend him, which was a completely ridiculous reaction, one she quickly squashed.

"I've been lied to so many times. I don't know if I forgive that."

"You're the only one who can decide that, honey," Julia said, squeezing her fingers. "But whatever you do, you know we're behind you, right?"

"Ditto from the Patagonia faction," Sage said over the phone.

Though she was quite certain it was watery and weak, Anna managed a smile. "Thank you. Thank you both. As tough as this is, I'm grateful I have you both."

"And Conan and Abigail," Sage declared. "Don't forget them."

The dog slapped his tail on the floor at the sound of his name but didn't bother getting up.

"How can I?" she said. She and Julia were saying goodbye and preparing to hang up when Sage suddenly gasped into the phone.

"The letter! We've got a letter for Abigail's nephew, remember?"

"That's right," Anna exclaimed. "I completely forgot it!"

"What letter?" Julia asked.

"From Abigail," Anna explained. "She left it as part of her estate papers for her great-nephew. Her Jamie."

"It was another of those weird conditions of her will," Sage added. "He could only receive it if and when he arrived in person to Brambleberry House. I was all in favor of mailing it to him in care of the army but Abigail's attorney stipulated her wishes were quite clear. We weren't even supposed to tell him about it until he showed up here."

"Why was she so certain he would come back to Brambleberry House after her death? Especially since she had gone to such pains to leave the house to you two, leaving him with no reason to return at all?" Julia asked with a puzzled frown.

"I don't know. I wondered that myself," Anna admitted.

She remembered how sad she had thought it that Abigail seemed so desperate for her nephew, who hadn't visited her much when she was alive, to come here, even after her death.

"She was right though," Sage said. "Just like she always was. He came back, just as she seemed to know he would."

Anna shivered at the undeniable truth of the words.

"You have to give it to him," Sage continued. "Do you know where it is?"

"In the safe in my office," she answered promptly. "I kept it there with all the other estate documents."

"I'd give anything to know what's in that letter. What do you think Abigail had to say to him?" Sage asked.

Anna wondered the same thing after she and Julia had said goodbye to Sage and she had returned downstairs to her own apartment and retrieved the letter from her safe.

She sat looking at the envelope for a long time, at Abigail's familiar elegant handwriting and those two words. *My Jamie.*

For the first time, she allowed herself to look at this from Max's perspective. He said he had loved his aunt and she knew she had hurt him tonight when she said Abigail must not have loved him enough to leave the house to him.

It had been a cruel thing to say, especially since she knew from the way Abigail talked about her nephew that she had adored him.

What would Anna have done if a beloved elderly relative had left a valuable legacy to two strangers? She probably would have been suspicious as well. Of course, she would have wanted to find out the circumstances. But would she have lied about her identity to investigate?

She couldn't answer that. She only knew that some of her anger seemed to be subsiding, drawing away from her like low tide.

She gazed at the letter. *My Jamie.* She was going to have to give it to him, but she knew she couldn't go knocking on his apartment door. She wasn't ready to face him again. Not yet. Maybe in the morning, she would be more in control of her emotions.

Still, some instinct told her she needed to deliver this tonight, whether she faced him or not. Praying she wouldn't encounter him wandering around in the dark, she moved quietly up the stairs and slipped the letter through the narrow crack under the door.

There you go, Abigail, she thought, and was almost certain she felt a brush of air against her cheek.

The task done, she stood for a long moment on the landing outside his apartment, her emotions a tangled mess and her heart a heavy weight in her chest.

Max backed his SUV out of the Brambleberry House driveway just as the sun crested the coast range. His duffel and single suitcase were in the backseat and the letter that had been slipped under his apartment door was on the seat beside him.

He knew the letter was from Abigail. Who else? Even if he hadn't recognized her distinctive curlicue handwriting, he would have known from only the name on the outside.

My Jamie.

He had stared at that envelope, his heart aching with loss and regret. It even smelled like her, some soft, flowery scent that made him think of tight hugs and kisses on the cheek and summer evening spent in the garden with her.

Finally he had stuck it in the pocket of his jacket and walked down the stairs of Brambleberry House for the last time.

He knew of only one place he wanted to be when he read her final words to him. It seemed fitting and right that he drive to the cemetery to pay his last respects before he left Cannon Beach. He had been putting it off, this final evidence that Abigail was really gone, but he knew he couldn't avoid the inevitable any longer.

He found the cemetery and drove through the massive iron gates under winter-bare branches. Only when he was inside looking at the rows of gravestones, surrounded by tendrils of misty morning fog, did he realize he had no idea where to find his aunt's plot amid the graves.

At random, he picked a lane and parked his SUV halfway down it then started walking. He had only gone twenty feet before he saw it, a tasteful headstone in pale amber marble under a small statue of an angel, with her name.

Abigail Elizabeth Dandridge

Someone had angled an intricate wrought-iron bench there to look over the grave and the ocean beyond it. Anna? he wondered. Somehow it wouldn't have surprised him. It seemed the sort of gesture she would make, practical and softhearted at the same time.

He sat at the bench for a long time, until the damp grass began to seep through his boots and the wrought-iron pressed into the back of his thighs. He wasn't quite sure why he was so apprehensive to read Abigail's final words to him.

Maybe because of that—because it seemed so very final. Silly as it seemed, he hated that this was the last time anyone would call him the nickname only she had used.

Finally he opened the envelope. A tiny key fell out, along with several pieces of cream vellum. He frowned and pocketed the key then unfolded the letter, his insides twisting.

My dear Jamie,
I suppose since you're reading this, it means you have come home to Brambleberry House at last. I say home, my dear, because this is where you have always belonged. During the rough years of your childhood, while you were off at military school, even when you were off serving your country with honor and courage, this was your home. You have always had a home here and I hope with all my heart that you have known that.
By now you must be thinking I'm a crazy old bat. I'm not so sure you would be wrong. I want you to

know I'm a crazy old bat who has loved you dearly. You have been my joy every day of your life.

So why didn't I leave you the house? I'm sure you're asking. If you're not, you should be. I nearly did, you know. Since the day you were born, I planned that you would inherit Brambleberry House when I left this earth. Then a few years ago, something happened to change my mind.

I began to want something more for you than just a house. You see, houses get dry rot or are bent and broken by the wind or can even crumble into the ocean.

Love, though. Love endures.

I knew love when I was a girl, a love that stayed with me my entire life. Even though the man I loved died young, I have carried the memory of him inside me all these years. It has sustained me and lifted me throughout my life's journey.

I wanted the same for you, my Jamie. For you to know the connection of two hearts linked as one. So I began to scheme and to plot. You needed a special woman, someone smart and courageous, with a strong, loving heart.

I knew from the moment I met Anna, she was perfect for you.

He stopped and stared at the gravestone as a chill rippled down his spine. Impossible. How could Abigail have known from beyond the grave that he would find Anna, that he would fall in love with her, that he would feel as if his heart were being ripped out of him at the idea of walking away from her? With numb disbelief, he turned his attention back to the letter.

I wanted you to meet her, Jamie. To see for yourself how wonderful she is. I thought if I left you the house outright, you would quickly sell it and return to the army, leaving all you could have found here behind without a backward glance.

Anna and Sage would watch over my house with loving care, I knew. And I also knew that if I left the house to them, eventually you would come home to find out why. I thought perhaps when you did, you would find something far more valuable here than bricks and drywall and a leaky roof.

It was a gamble—a huge one. I only wish I could be there to see if it paid out. Of course, there was always a chance you might fall for Sage, but I had other plans for her, plans that didn't include you.

I can't even contemplate the eventuality that you might not fall for Anna. You are too smart for that—or at least you'd better be!

Please know that my dearest wish is that you will find joy, my darling Jamie.

All my love, forever,

Abigail.

P.S. In case you're wondering, the key is to a safe-deposit box at First National Bank of Oregon where you will find record of my investment portfolio. The proceeds are all to go to you, as the legal documentation in the safe deposit will attest and my attorney can confirm. I've played the market well over the years and I believe you'll find the value of my portfolio far exceeds the worth of an old rambling house on the seashore. I pray you will put my money to good use somewhere, even if I'm wrong about you and Anna being perfect for each other.

He stared at the letter for a long, long time, there in the cemetery with only the wind sighing in the trees and a pair of robins singing and flitting from branch to branch as they prepared their spring nest.

All these years, he had no idea his great-aunt was a sly, manipulative rascal.

He ought to be angry at her for luring him here. She had set him up, had played him every step of the way.

Instead, he laughed out loud, then couldn't seem to stop. He laughed so hard the robins fluttered into the sky, chattering angrily at him for disturbing their work.

"Oh, Abigail," he said out loud. "You are one in a million."

How could he be angry, when her actions had been motivated only by love for him? And when she was absolutely right?

Anna was a smart, courageous woman with a strong, loving heart. And she was perfect for him.

He couldn't just walk away from her, from the chance to see if he could find what Abigail wanted so much for them both.

He was gone.

Anna sat on the porch swing where Max had held her so tenderly the night of the storm and gazed out at the sleeping garden, at the rose bushes with their naked thorns and the dry husks of daylily leaves she hadn't cut down in the fall and the bare dirt that waited in a state of anticipation for what was to come.

He was gone and she was quite certain he wouldn't be back. His SUV was gone when she awoke and when she had let Conan out, she had found the key to his apartment hanging on her doorknob, along with a simple note.

I'm so sorry, he had written, without even signing his name.

The morning was cold, with wisps of fog coming off the sea to curl through the trees and around the garden. She shivered from it. She really should go inside and get ready for work but she couldn't seem to move from the porch swing.

Conan, his eyes deep with concern, padded to her and placed his head in her lap.

Just that tiny gesture of comfort sent the first tear trickling down her cheek, then another and another until she buried her face in her hands and wept.

She gave into the storm of emotions for only a few moments before she straightened and drew in a shaky breath, swiping at the tears on her cheeks. Of course he was gone. What did she expect? She had made it quite clear to him the night before that she couldn't forgive him for lying to her. Did she expect him to stick around hoping she would change her mind?

Would she have?

It was a question she didn't know the answer to. This morning, her anger had faded, leaving only an echo of hurt that he had maintained the deception even after they made love.

Julia's words kept running through her head.

Maybe he just found himself in a deep hole and he didn't know how to climb out without digging in deeper.

Yes, he had lied about his identity. But she couldn't quite believe everything else was a lie. He had stood up to Grayson for her that day in the store, he had come with her to the verdict, had held her hand when she was afraid, had kissed her with stunning tenderness. What was truth and what was a lie?

She loved him. That, at least, was undeniably true.

She let out one last sob, her hands buried in Conan's fur, then she straightened her spine. He was gone and she could do nothing about it. In the meantime, she had two businesses to run and a house to take care of. And now she needed to find a new tenant for her third-floor apartment so she could pay for a new roof.

Conan suddenly jerked away from her and went to the edge of the porch, barking wildly. She turned to see what had captured his attention and her heart stuttered in her chest.

Max walked toward her through the morning mist, looking lean and masculine and dangerous in his leather bomber jacket with his arm in the sling.

The breath caught in her throat as he walked toward her and stopped a half-dozen feet away.

"I made you cry."

"No, you didn't. I never cry."

He raised an eyebrow and she lifted her chin defiantly. "It's just cold out here and my allergies must be starting up. It's early spring and the grass pollen count is probably sky-high."

Now who was lying? she thought, clamping her teeth together before she could ramble on more and make things worse.

"Is that right?" he murmured, though he didn't look as if he believed her for an instant.

"I thought you left," she said after a moment.

He shrugged. "I came back."

"You left your key and vacated the apartment."

Where did this cool, composed voice of hers come from? she wondered. What she really wanted to do instead of standing out here having such a civil conversation was to leap into his arms and hold on tight.

He shrugged, leaning a hip against the carved porch support post. "I changed my mind. I don't want to leave."

"Too bad. You can't walk out on a lease agreement and then waltz back in just because you feel like it."

Amusement sparked in his hazel eyes. Amusement and something else, something that had her pulse racing. "Are you going to take me to court, Anna? Because I have to tell you, that would look pretty bad for you. I would hate to pull out the pity card but I just don't see how you could avoid the ugly headlines. 'Vindictive landlady kicks out injured war veteran.'"

She bristled. "Vindictive? *Vindictive?*"

"Okay, bad choice of words. How about, 'Justifiably angry landlady.'"

"Better."

"No, wait. I've got the perfect headline." He slid away from the post and stepped closer and her pulse kicked up a dozen notches at the intent look in his eyes.

"How about 'Idiotic injured soldier falls hard for lovely landlady.'"

"Because only an idiot would be stupid enough to fall for her, right?"

He laughed roughly. "You're not going to make this easy on me, are you?"

She shrugged instead of answering, mostly because she didn't quite trust her voice.

Just kiss me already.

"All right, this is my last attempt here. How about 'Ex-helicopter pilot loses heart to successful local business owner, declares he can't live without her.'"

Conan barked suddenly with delight and Anna could only stare at Max, her heart pounding so loudly she was quite certain he must be able to hear it. She didn't know quite how to adjust to the quicksilver shift from despair to this bright, vibrant joy bursting through her.

"I like it," she whispered. "No, I love it."

He grinned suddenly and she thought again how much he had changed in the short time he'd been at Brambleberry House.

"It's a keeper then," he said, then he finally stepped forward and kissed her with fierce tenderness.

Tears welled up in her eyes again, this time tears of joy, and she returned his kiss with all the emotion in her heart.

"Can you forgive me, Anna? I made a mistake. I should never have tried to deceive you and I certainly shouldn't have played it out so long. I never expected to fall in love with you. That wasn't in the plan—or at least not in *my* plan."

"Whose plan was it?"

"I've got something to show you. Something I'm quite sure you're not going to believe."

He eased onto the porch swing and pulled her onto his lap as if he couldn't bear to let her go. She was going to be late for work, Anna thought, but right now she didn't give a darn. She didn't want to be anywhere else in the world but right here, in the arms of the man she loved.

"I'm assuming you're the one who slipped the letter from Aunt Abigail under my door."

She nodded. "She was quite strict in her instructions that you not receive it until you returned to Brambleberry House in person. Sage and I didn't understand it but the attorney said that was nonnegotiable."

"That's because she was manipulating us all," he answered. "Here. See for yourself."

He handed her the letter and she scanned the words with growing astonishment. By the time she was done, a single tear dripped down the side of her nose.

"The wretch," she exclaimed, then she laughed out loud. "How could she possibly know?"

"What? That you're perfect for me?"

Her gaze flashed to his and she saw blazing emotion there that sent heat and that wild flutter of joy coursing through her. "Am I?" she whispered, afraid to believe it.

"You are everything I never knew I needed, Anna. I

love you. With everything inside me, I love you. Abigail got that part exactly right."

She wanted to cry again. To laugh and cry and hold him close.

Thank you, Abigail. For this wonderful gift, thank you from the bottom of my heart.

"Oh, Max. I love you. I think I fell in love with you that first morning on the beach when you were so kind to Conan."

He kissed her, his mouth tender and his eyes filled with emotion. "I'm not the poetry type of guy, Anna. But I can tell you that my heart definitely found a home here, and not because of the house. Because of you."

This time her tears slipped through and she wrapped her arms around him, holding tight.

Just before he kissed her, Anna could swear she heard a sigh of satisfied delight. She opened her eyes and was quite certain that over his shoulder she caught the glitter of an ethereal kind of shadow drifting through the garden, past the edge of the yard and on toward the beach.

She blinked again and then it was gone.

She must have been mistaken, she thought, except Conan stood at the edge of the porch, looking in the same direction, his ears cocked.

The dog bounded down the steps and into the garden. He barked once, still looking out to sea.

After a long moment, he barked again, then gave that silly canine grin of his and returned to the porch to curl up at their feet.

Epilogue

It was easy to believe in happy endings at a moment like this.

Max sat in the gardens of Brambleberry House on a lovely June day. The wild riot of colorful flowers gleamed in the late-afternoon sunlight and the air was scented with their perfume—roses and daylilies and the sweet, seductive smell of lavender that melded with the brisk, salty undertone of the sea.

Julia Blair was a beautiful bride. Her eyes were bright with happiness as she stood beside Will Garrett under an arbor covered in Abigail's favorite yellow roses while they exchanged vows.

The two of them were deeply in love and everyone at the wedding could see it. Max was glad for Will. He had been given a small glimpse from Abigail's letters over the years of how dark and desolate his friend's life had been after the deaths of his wife and daughter. These last three months,

Anna had shared a little more of Will's grieving process with Max and he couldn't imagine that kind of pain.

From what he could tell, Julia was the ideal woman to help Will move forward. Max had come to know her well after three months of living upstairs from her. She was sweet and compassionate, with a deep reservoir of love inside her that she showered on Will and her children.

"May I have the rings, please?" the pastor performing the ceremony asked. Then he had to repeat his request since Simon, the ring bearer and best man, was busy making faces at Chloe Spencer.

"Simon, pay attention," his twin sister hissed loudly. To emphasize her point, she poked him hard with the basket full of the flower petals she had strewn along the garden path before the ceremony.

"Sorry," Simon muttered, then held the pillow holding the rings out to Will, who was doing his best to fight a smile.

"Thanks, bud," Will said, reaching for the rings with one hand while he squeezed the boy's shoulder with the other in a man-to-man kind of gesture.

As Will and Julia exchanged rings, Max heard a small sniffle beside him and turned his head to find Anna's brown eyes shimmering with tears she tried hard to contain.

He curled his fingers more tightly around hers, and as she leaned her cheek against his shoulder for just a moment, he was astounded all over again at how very much his world had changed in just a few short months.

She had become everything to him.

His love.

When the clergyman pronounced them man and wife and they kissed to seal their union, he watched as the tears Anna had been fighting broke free and started to trickle down her cheek.

He pulled a handkerchief from the pocket of his dress

uniform, and she dabbed at her eyes. For a woman who claimed she never cried, she had become remarkably proficient at it.

She had cried a month earlier when Sage Benedetto-Spencer told them she and Eben were expecting a baby, due exactly on Abigail's birthday in November.

She'd cried the day the accountant at her Lincoln City store told her they were safely in the black after several record months of sales.

And she had cried buckets for him when, after his latest trip to Walter Reed a month ago, he had come to the inevitable conclusion that he couldn't keep trying to pretend everything would be all right with his shoulder; when he had finally accepted he would never be able to fly a helicopter again.

Max could have left the army completely at that point on a medical discharge, but he had opted instead only to leave active duty. Serving part-time in the army reserves based out of Portland would be a different challenge for him, but he knew he still had much to offer.

The ceremony ended and the newly married couple was immediately surrounded by well-wishers—Conan at the front of the pack. Though he had waited with amazing patience through the service, sitting next to Sage in the front row, the dog apparently had decided he needed to be in the middle of the action.

Conan looked only slightly disgruntled at the bow tie he had been forced to wear. Maybe he knew he'd gotten a lucky reprieve—Julia's twins had pleaded for a full tuxedo for him but Anna had talked them out of it, much to Conan's relief, Max was quite certain.

"What a gorgeous day for a party." Sage Benedetto-Spencer approached them with her husband. "The garden looks spectacular. I've never seen the colors so rich."

"Your husband's landscape crew from the Sea Urchin did most of the work," Anna said.

"Not true," Eben piped in, wrapping his arms around his wife. "I have it on good authority that you and Max had already done most of the hard work by the time they got here."

Max considered the long evenings and weekends they had spent preparing the yard for the ceremony as a gift—to himself, most of all. Here in Abigail's lush gardens as they'd pruned and planted, he and Anna had talked and laughed and kissed and enjoyed every moment of being together.

He loved watching her, elbow-deep in dirt, Abigail's floppy hat on as she lifted her face to the evening sunshine.

Okay, he loved watching her do anything. Whether it was flying kites with the twins on the beach or throwing a stick for Conan in the yard or sitting at her office desk, her brow wrinkled with concentration as she reconciled her accounts.

He was just plain crazy about her.

They spoke for a few more moments with Eben and Sage before Anna excused herself to make certain the caterers were ready to start bringing out the appetizers for the reception.

When she still hadn't returned a half hour later, Max went searching for her.

He found her alone in the kitchen of her apartment, which had been set up as food central, setting bacon-wrapped shrimp on etched silver platters. Typical Anna, he thought with a grin. Sure, the caterer Julia and Will had hired was probably more than capable of handling all these little details, but she must be busy somewhere else and Anna must have stepped in to help. She loved being involved in the action. If there was work to be done, his Anna didn't hesitate.

She was humming to herself, and he listened to her for a moment, admiring the brisk efficiency of her movements, then he slid in behind her with as much stealth as he could manage. She wore her hair up and he couldn't resist leaning forward and brushing a kiss along the elegant arch of her bared neck, just on the spot he had learned, these last few months, was most sensitive.

A delicate shiver shook her frame and her hands paused in their work. "I don't know who you are, but don't stop," she purred in a low, throaty voice.

He laughed and turned her to face him. She raised her eyebrows in a look of mock surprise as she slid into his arms. "Oh. Max. Hi."

He kissed her properly this time, astonished all over again at the little bump in his pulse, at the love that swelled inside him whenever he had her in his arms.

"It's been a beautiful day, hasn't it?" she said, soft joy in her eyes for her friends' happiness.

"Beautiful," he agreed, without a trace of the cynicism he had expected.

His own mother had been married six times, the most recent just a few weeks ago to some man she'd met on a three-week Mediterranean cruise. With his childhood and the examples he had seen, he had always considered the idea of happy endings like Julia and Will's—and Sage and Eben's, for that matter—just another fairy tale. But this time with her had changed everything.

"Anna, I want this," he said suddenly.

"The shrimp? I know, they're divine, aren't they? I think I could eat the whole platter myself."

"Not the shrimp. I want the whole thing. The wedding, the flowers. The crazy-spooky dog with the bow tie. I want all of it."

She blinked rapidly, and he saw color soak her cheeks. "Oh," she said slowly.

He wasn't going about this the right way at all. He had

a feeling if Abigail happened to be watching she would be laughing her head off just about now at how inept he was.

"I'm sorry I don't have all the flowery words. I only know that I love you with everything inside me. I want forever, Anna." He paused, his heartbeat sounding unnaturally loud in his ears. "Will you marry me?"

She gazed at him for a long, drawn-out moment. Through the open window behind her, he was vaguely aware of the band starting up, playing something soft and slow and romantic.

"Oh, Max," she said. She sniffled once, then again, then she threw herself back into his arms.

"Yes. Yes, yes, yes," she laughed, punctuating each word with a kiss.

"A smart businesswoman like you had better think this through before you answer so definitively. I'm not much of a bargain, I'm afraid. Are you really sure you'll be happy married to a weekend warrior and high-school physics teacher who's greener at his new job than a kid on his first day of basic training?"

"I don't need to think anything through. I love you, Max. I want the whole thing, too." She kissed him again. "And besides, you're going to be a wonderful teacher."

Of all the careers out there, he never would have picked teaching for himself, but now it seemed absolutely right. He had always enjoyed giving training to new recruits and had been damn good at it. But high-school students? That was an entirely different matter.

Anna had been the one who'd pointed out to him how important the teachers at the military school Meredith sent him to had been in shaping his life and the man he had become. They'd been far more instrumental than his own mother.

Once the idea had been planted, it stuck. Since he already had a physics degree, now he only had to finish obtaining a teaching certificate. This time next year, he would be preparing lesson plans.

It wasn't the path he had expected, but that particular route had been blown apart by a rocket-fired grenade in Iraq. Somehow this one suddenly seemed exactly the right one for him.

He couldn't help remembering what Abigail used to say—*A bend in the road is only the end if you refuse to make the turn.* He was making the turn, and though he couldn't see it all clearly, he had a feeling the path ahead contained more joy than he could even imagine.

He rested his chin on Anna's hair. Already that joy seemed to seep through him, washing away all the pain. He couldn't wait to follow that road, to spend the rest of his life with efficient Anna—with her plans and her ambitions and her brilliant mind.

Suddenly, above the delectable smells of the wedding food, he was quite certain he smelled the sweet, summery scent of freesias.

"Do you think she's here today?" Anna asked him.

He tightened his arms around her, thinking of his aunt who had loved them all so much. "Absolutely," he murmured. "She wouldn't miss it. Just as I'm sure she'll be here for our wedding and for the birth of our children and for every step of our journey together."

Anna laughed softly. "We'd better hold on tight, then. If Abigail has her way, I think we're in for a wild ride. A wild, wonderful, perfect ride."

* * * * *

*Mills & Boon® Special Edition brings
you a sneak preview of…*

Gina Wilkins' The Man Next Door,
which is available in June 2009.

*Legal assistant Dani Madison had learned her
lesson about men the hard way. Or so she thought.
Because her irresistible new neighbour, FBI agent
Teague Carson, was about to show her playing it
safe would only take her so far…*

*Don't miss this exciting new story coming next
month in Mills & Boon® Special Edition!*

The Man Next Door

by

Gina Wilkins

Teague McCauley was so tired his steps dragged as he made his way from the parking lot to his apartment. It was actually an effort to place one foot in front of the other. He could feel his shoulders drooping. Even his dark hair felt limp around his face.

Though he usually took the stairs, he rode the elevator up to his third-floor apartment. He was the only occupant, since most of the other residents had already left for their jobs at eight-forty-five on this Tuesday morning. It would probably be quiet during the day as he got some sleep for the first time in more than forty-eight hours. Not that it would matter. He felt as though he could sleep in a blasting zone right now.

The elevator stopped and he pushed himself away from the wall he'd been leaning against. A few more steps, he reminded himself as the doors began to slide open, and then he could...

At the sight of the woman waiting for the elevator, he snapped instinctively to attention. He pulled his shoulders back, lifted his head and tightened his face into what he hoped was a pleasantly bland expression, nodding as he moved out of her way. "Good morning."

She looked as fresh as a fall chrysanthemum in a bright orange top and crisp brown slacks, her long, glossy brown hair shining around her pretty oval face, her navy-blue eyes cool when she returned the greeting perfunctorily. "Good morning."

"Have a nice day," he said over his shoulder as he strolled away, his steps brisk.

"You, too," she murmured, her reply as meaningless as the clichéd phrase that was all that had popped into his exhaustion-hazed mind.

He heard the elevator doors swish closed behind him, and his back sagged again, his feet almost stumbling the rest of the way to his apartment door. *Yeah,* he thought, fumbling with the key, *you really wowed her with your witty conversation, McCauley.*

Not that it would have mattered if he had come up with even the most clever line. His down-the-hall neighbor had made it very clear during the past few months that she wasn't interested in getting to know him better. Something about the way she practically glowered at him every time she saw him, not to mention the ice that dripped from her tone every time he manipulated her into speaking to him, as he had just then, had given him a clue.

As an FBI agent, he liked to think he was pretty good at reading between the lines that way.

It was a shame, really, he thought, already stripping out of his black T-shirt as he headed straight toward his bedroom without even bothering to turn on lights in the spartanly furnished living room. She certainly was a looker. Face of an angel, body of a goddess. And all the warmth of a snow queen.

Totally out of clichés, he kicked his jeans into a corner, stripped off his socks and fell facedown onto his bed, wearing nothing but navy boxers. He didn't have time for a relationship, anyway, he thought as consciousness began to fade.

Still a shame, though…

Dani Madison waited until she was certain the elevator doors were closed before she released the long breath she'd been holding. It was the same every time she ran into the man who lived in the apartment down the hall. Her breath caught, her pulse tripped, little nerve endings all over her body woke up and started tingling. Very annoying.

Fortunately, she rarely saw him. Maybe a half dozen times total, in the approximately four months since he'd moved in. He wasn't home much, being gone sometimes for more than a week at a time, from what she'd observed. When he was home, it was at strange hours. Like today, just coming in when most people were leaving for work. Looking so tired she'd thought it was a wonder he was standing upright, even though he'd made an obvious, macho effort to hide his exhaustion.

He worked for the FBI. She knew that because he occasionally wore T-shirts with the letters stenciled across his chest. Sometimes he wore suits, and she thought she'd caught a glimpse of a holster beneath his jacket. Maybe that was part of the reason she found him so intriguing.

Well, that and the fact that he was absolutely, positively, heart-stoppingly attractive. Black hair worn a bit shaggy. Gray eyes that looked almost silver at times. Straight, dark eyebrows, neat, midlength sideburns, a jawline that could have been chiseled from granite, but with just a hint of a dimple in his right cheek to add a touch of softness. When he was unshaven, as he had been this morning, he had the look of a pirate or an Old West lawman. A little wild, a little danger-ous—a whole boatload of sexy.

All added together, those things were enough to make her feel the need to run very hard in the opposite direction every time she saw him.

Not that he would bother to pursue her if she did, she thought, shifting her leather tote bag on her shoulder as she stepped off the elevator. Other than greeting her politely each time they passed in the hallway, he'd shown no particular interest in her. Mrs. Parsons, the nosy little old lady who lived in the apartment next door to hers, directly across from the man in question, showed more curiosity about her. Agent Double-O Gorgeous had barely even noticed her.

Exactly the way she wanted things to remain, she assured herself. She had spent the past fourteen months avoiding any complicated entanglements with men, most especially the dangerous-looking ones. And her FBI neighbor sat firmly at the very top of that list.

It had taken her more than twenty-seven years and a long, humiliating list of mistakes, but she had finally learned her lesson, she thought with a sense of accomplishment. Dani Madison was on her own, independent, self-sufficient, cau-tious and wisely cynical. It was going to take more than a rolling swagger and a pair of gleaming silver eyes to change her back into the naive and affection-hungry girl she had been before.

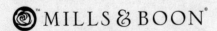

In the Sheikh's power

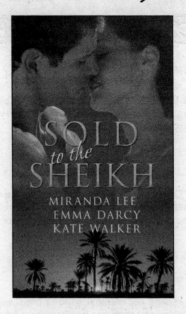

Be tempted by three seductive Sheikhs in:

Love-Slave to the Sheikh by Miranda Lee
Traded to the Sheikh by Emma Darcy
At the Sheikh's Command by Kate Walker

Available 5th June 2009

FREE

2 BOOKS AND A SURPRISE GIFT!

We would like to take this opportunity to thank you for reading this Mills & Boon® book by offering you the chance to take TWO more specially selected titles from the Special Edition series absolutely FREE! We're also making this offer to introduce you to the benefits of the Mills & Boon® Book Club™—

- ★ **FREE home delivery**
- ★ **FREE gifts and competitions**
- ★ **FREE monthly Newsletter**
- ★ **Books available before they're in the shops**
- ★ **Exclusive Mills & Boon Book Club offers**

Accepting these FREE books and gift places you under no obligation to buy; you may cancel at any time, even after receiving your free shipment. Simply complete your details below and return the entire page to the address below. You don't even need a stamp!

YES! Please send me 2 free Special Edition books and a surprise gift. I understand that unless you hear from me, I will receive 4 superb new titles every month for just £3.19 each, postage and packing free. I am under no obligation to purchase any books and may cancel my subscription at any time. The free books and gift will be mine to keep in any case.

E9ZEE

Ms/Mrs/Miss/Mr...Initials ....

BLOCK CAPITALS PLEASE

Surname ....

Address ....

....

....Postcode ....

Send this whole page to:

The Mills & Boon Book Club, FREEPOST CN81, Croydon, CR9 3WZ